KU-022-168

Was Sorrel planning to live in the house her godmother had left her?

His mouth sketched a cold smile. Not if he had any say in it.

The Sorrel with whom he'd shared a magical, innocent summer years before was long gone, transformed into a woman whose face had smiled with sultry aloofness in hundreds of magazines, finally starring in a perfume campaign that had raised eyebrows worldwide.

Sometimes Luke dreamed he was the man she was looking at, her slanted, sleepy eyes half closed in slumbrous invitation, her mouth parted and expectant.

Despising himself for the jolt of pure lust that tightened every muscle, he turned the wheel onto the bridge at Parenga and swore as he took the corner too fast. The lapse of concentration stung.

On the night before her eighteenth birthday she'd gazed up at him with exactly that smile. Goaded by the lash of a desire that had grown unbidden day after day, he'd kissed her. And nothing had ever been the same since.

Robyn Donald has always lived in Northland in New Zealand, initially on her father's stud dairy farm at Warkworth, then in the Bay of Islands, an area of great natural beauty, where she lives today with her husband and an ebullient and mostly Labrador dog. She resigned her teaching position when she fund she enjoyed writing romances more, and now spends any time not writing in reading, gardening, travelling and writing letters to keep up with her two adult children and her friends.

Recent titles by the same author:

THE PRINCE'S PLEASURE
WOLFE'S TEMPTRESS
FORGOTTEN SINS
THE DEVIL'S BARGAIN
A RUTHLESS PASSION

ONE NIGHT AT PARENGA

BY
ROBYN DONALD

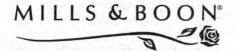

DID YOU PURCHASE THIS BOOK WITHOUT A COVER?

If you did, you should be aware it is **stolen property** as it was reported
unsold and destroyed by a retailer. Neither the author nor the publisher
has received any payment for this book.

*All the characters in this book have no existence outside the imagination
of the author, and have no relation whatsoever to anyone bearing the
same name or names. They are not even distantly inspired by any
individual known or unknown to the author, and all the incidents are
pure invention.*

*All Rights Reserved including the right of reproduction in whole or in
part in any form. This edition is published by arrangement with
Harlequin Enterprises II B.V. The text of this publication or any part
thereof may not be reproduced or transmitted in any form or by any
means, electronic or mechanical, including photocopying, recording,
storage in an information retrieval system, or otherwise, without the
written permission of the publisher.*

*This book is sold subject to the condition that it shall not, by way of
trade or otherwise, be lent, resold, hired out or otherwise circulated
without the prior consent of the publisher in any form of binding or
cover other than that in which it is published and without a similar
condition including this condition being imposed on the subsequent
purchaser.*

*MILLS & BOON and MILLS & BOON with the Rose Device
are registered trademarks of the publisher.*

*First published in Great Britain 2002
Harlequin Mills & Boon Limited,
Eton House, 18-24 Paradise Road, Richmond, Surrey TW9 1SR*

© Robyn Donald 2002

ISBN 0 263 83199 X

*Set in Times Roman 10½ on 12 pt.
01-0103-46096*

*Printed and bound in Spain
by Litografia Rosés, S.A., Barcelona*

PROLOGUE

'SO THERE'S nothing left,' Sorrel Maitland said almost soundlessly, her face a beautiful mask. New Zealand was a long way from New York, and she'd lived in the States for almost eight years, yet her low voice still carried the accent of her birth country.

The lawyer directed a keen glance at her, relieved when the huge gold-green eyes remained dry and tearless. 'Very little, I'm afraid.'

He saw her brace herself.

She said huskily, 'It was—a lot of money to lose. What happened to it?'

'It appears your father's a gambler, and that's a quick, easy way to lose money.' He glanced down at the documents on his desk. The several million Sorrel Maitland had earned over the past years had slipped through her father's fingers as easily as water cupped in a hand.

She scanned the figures he'd given her and asked a couple of pertinent questions.

Brains as well as beauty, he decided after he'd answered, admiring the magnificent red-brown sweep of hair pulled back in a sleek, sophisticated chignon.

Family loyalty could cause enormous problems, and sometimes outright disasters like this one. If she'd come to him at the start of her career he'd have warned her that parents are rarely the best protectors of their children's earnings, but what girl of eighteen would have believed that?

5

'I wish I had better news to give you,' he said.

He was even sorrier to shatter her illusions. It was difficult to feel much sympathy over the lost earnings, massive though they were. Although the woman seated on the other side of the desk wasn't one of the top ten supermodels, she was famous enough, and as she was only in her mid-twenties she had a few years yet to build up another nest egg.

Broken trust was another thing entirely.

He said, 'If gambling addicts don't get help they subordinate everything—honesty, faith, the people they love—to the compulsion. An alcoholic needs support and a huge amount of will-power to overcome the need to drink, and it's the same for a gambling addiction. Some people won't admit to a problem, and others try, but can't get it under control.'

Almost noiselessly she said, 'I knew he enjoyed a flutter at the casino, and that he bet on horses, but—' She stopped, then finished helplessly, 'I had no idea.'

'Usually the families don't, until something like this happens.' He leaned forward. 'Ms Maitland, you must put your affairs in other hands.'

'I will. I know you and your staff have put in impossibly long hours to untangle my father's and my affairs,' she said quietly, her voice even and unemotional. 'Thank you for working so hard.'

'You're very welcome,' he said awkwardly. 'If there's any advice I can give, all you have to do is ask.'

Tall and impossibly elegant, she rose in a fluid motion and held out her hand. The legendary smile lit up her face, its slow radiance barely dimmed.

'You're very kind, but I know what to do now.'

Afterwards he wondered why he'd shaken her hand so carefully—as though she might break. However, her grip had been steady and firm, only the chill of her long fingers revealing the turmoil behind the smooth, immaculately made-up features and the formal words.

A class act, he thought as he closed the door of his office behind her.

An almost bankrupt class act.

In the apartment she'd shared with her father, Sorrel took off her gloves and walked across to the window to stare down at the snow-covered spread of Central Park.

Swivelling away, she pressed the heels of her hands into her burning eyes, holding the tears back until coloured sparks danced against her lids. In the space of a month her life had splintered, its jagged fragments impossible to reassemble.

First her beloved godmother's death in New Zealand, and hard on that shock had come the stroke that had imprisoned her father in the wreckage of his own body. Cynthia's house, Parenga, was empty, but her father was still alive.

If you could call his existence living.

Sorrel dropped her hands and blinked for several moments to bring the world into focus. A rapid glance at her watch told her she had half an hour before it was time to go back to the very expensive nursing home that would be Nigel Maitland's home for the foreseeable future.

But, as one of the things he'd failed to do was set up medical insurance for himself, she had to ring her agent first.

'Louise,' she said briskly. 'About the Founiere offer—I'll take it.'

Louise gave a small, hastily silenced shriek. 'Honey,

that's great news. Belle Sandford got her start in one of their campaigns, and I just heard today she's a cert for an Oscar nomination. Founiere are a fabulous firm for publicity—they're really proud of their reputation for exotic good taste.'

'Or tasteful exotica,' Sorrel said drily, thinking that *erotica* was a much better word for the perfume campaigns run by the world-famous cosmetic firm.

Her super-sharp agent snorted. 'Prissy, prissy, prissy, Sorrel! If you still think Founiere do soft porn, what changed your mind?'

The money from that campaign would keep her father in the clinic. Not that she was going to tell Louise that—the fewer people who knew about her situation the better.

'I just thought it might be fun—and different.' Her voice sounded thin and squeezed of emotion. She swallowed and forced a note of enthusiasm into her words. 'And, as you say, it might lead to—other things.'

'OK.' Louise's voice altered. 'I'm really glad you've made this decision—it's probably your last chance with Founiere. You're still gorgeous, of course, but I'd be failing as your agent if I didn't warn you that there are plenty ready to take your place.'

'A whole world of beautiful, hungry sixteen-year-olds,' Sorrel said lightly. 'It's all right, Louise, I know the life expectancy of models.'

'Well, you've got a few years in hand yet,' Louise reassured her. 'You take care, now. I'll be in touch.'

Sorrel hung up and looked around the apartment. It would have to go. Fortunately she had no emotional ties to the place—it had been her father's choice.

In the kitchen she poured a glass of water and drank it down before walking into the room her father called his office. Like him, it was organised and tidy; he'd kept the details of all his debts with compulsive neatness.

She tried to reconcile the father she'd known and loved all her life with the man who'd stripped her of nearly every cent to feed his gambling habit, but her brain couldn't cope.

Whatever, he was her father and he loved her. Perhaps more important, he needed her; although he could only move one eyelid, the nurses said his vital signs improved when she came in and deteriorated when she left. She had to find the money to pay for his care until…

'Until he gets better,' she said sturdily, knowing that he'd almost certainly never improve.

Her vital, energetic, vigorous father had nothing but misery to look forward to. So, if keeping him comfortable and cared for meant posing half-naked in a series of 'tasteful' perfume ads, she'd do it.

She couldn't afford the luxury of finer feelings.

CHAPTER ONE

LUKE HARDCASTLE strode across the forecourt outside Waimanu homestead, black brows drawing together in his hard, handsome face as his housekeeper looked at him with something like appeal. With her was the driver of a truck from the local carriers, and by her stance she appeared to be arguing with him.

'What's the problem?' Luke demanded.

Both turned to him with evident relief, speaking at the same time. 'Penn,' he decided, and the driver fell silent.

His housekeeper shot a disparaging look at the man. 'He says he has a box for Sorrel Maitland at Parenga, and I'm trying to tell him she doesn't live there.' She explained as though to a child, 'The Bannings rented the house for two years after Mrs Copestake died, but they shifted to Taupo a couple of weeks ago. Parenga's empty now.'

The driver said bluntly, 'I've been into Parenga and seen that nobody's living there now, but the directions on the box are plain—Sorrel Maitland, Parenga, Hardcastle Road—and that's where I have to leave it.'

Luke resisted the fierce clamour of sensation roaring through his big body. God, was it never going to end?

For ten years Sorrel had haunted him, filling him with frustration and anger. He'd despised himself for following her progress through the raffish world she'd made her own, relieved when the alluring, sexy photographs and the endless, titillating allusions in gossip columns had stopped two years ago, after hints of a marriage, of drug abuse, of pregnancy.

It had almost been a relief to think of her as married.

Nevertheless, he couldn't prevent a harsh note of authority to his voice. 'Can't you take it back to the depot until it's collected?'

In an aggrieved tone the driver told him, 'I've already rung the boss, but he says we haven't got the space to keep it until this Sorrel Maitland turns up. And I can't just dump it at Parenga—as far as I can see there's no place to store it out of the weather. Anyway, someone's got to sign for it.'

Crisply Luke said, 'I've got a key to Parenga—I'll follow you back there and we'll put it in the house.' From the corner of his eye he saw his housekeeper's mouth open. 'Thank you, Penn.'

She flushed a little, nodding before walking stiff-backed through the door and closing it with a slight bang behind her. Luke swung into his Land Rover and headed off behind the truck.

Was Sorrel planning to live in the house her god-mother had left her?

His mouth sketched a cold smile. Not if he had any say in it.

The Sorrel with whom he'd shared a magical, innocent summer years before was long gone, transformed into the woman whose face had smiled with sultry aloofness in hundreds of magazines, finally starring in a perfume campaign that had raised eyebrows worldwide.

Sometimes Luke dreamed he was the man she was looking at, her slanted, sleepy eyes half closed in slumbrous invitation, her mouth parted and expectant.

Despising himself for the jolt of pure lust that tightened every muscle, he turned the car onto the bridge at Parenga and swore as he took the corner too fast. The Land Rover coped, of course, clattering over the side-less wooden decking, but the lapse of concentration stung.

On the night before her eighteenth birthday she'd gazed up at him with exactly that smile. Goaded by the lash of a desire that had grown unbidden day after day, he'd kissed her.

And nothing had ever been the same since.

He'd known then that he had to get rid of Sorrel, and with ruthless determination he'd done it; he didn't regret his actions for a moment, even though she still had the power to fill his dreams with thwarted, hungry passion.

So was she bringing the husband with her, or had she left him? Was there a husband? The fact that she was still Sorrel Maitland indicated not, but plenty of women kept their maiden name.

Hell, what did he care?

He pulled up on the gravel forecourt behind the truck. Although a man came in twice a month to keep the place tidy, the big Edwardian house where he'd been born dreamed lonely, wistful dreams in a garden clouded by solitude.

The waiting driver thrust his clipboard at him. 'I know who you are, and so does the boss, but rules are rules. We need to prove delivery.'

Luke scrawled a signature along the bottom of the form. 'How big is this box?'

'Size of a tea chest,' the driver said cheerfully. 'Not too heavy, though. Probably clothes. She's a model, isn't she, Sorrel Maitland?'

There was nothing leering or suggestive about his

words or tone, but Luke had to deliberately rein in a brusque reply. 'She used to be,' he said neutrally.

The truck driver grinned. 'Must be a looker, then.' Abashed by the swift blue glitter in Luke's grey gaze, he hastily returned the clipboard to the cab of his truck, saying too heartily, 'Well, we'd better get this inside.'

Later that night Luke stood at the window of his sitting room, icy eyes seeing nothing of the river estuary below the wide stretch of lawn and garden.

On the edge of his vision glimmered the provocative, sophisticated smile he'd seen more times than he could count. Just to remind himself of what she was, he'd looked the magazine out when he'd come in after a hard afternoon drafting cattle—working off, he admitted reluctantly, the chaotic emotions caused by the prospect of Sorrel's return.

On the cover she was elegant and provocative in the sort of gown women wore to balls—a sensuous slither of amber silk; inside, the advertisement revealed a different Sorrel. With an exclamation of disgust Luke picked up his untouched glass of whisky.

Sometimes he thought he'd never be able to chisel that bloody picture out of his brain. Oh, it was tasteful and beautiful, brilliantly lit and photographed, airbrushed to perfection...and sinfully erotic. Two gleaming, apparently naked bodies pressed in a sultry embrace, the man's hand almost touching the woman's breast as he gazed possessively into eyes that beckoned with a gleaming, sensuous promise, pale eyes with soft gold-green centres set off by a thin, stark rim the colour of black jade.

Cat's eyes, set on a slant, smoky with the promise of passion...

Whisky slid with raw impact down Luke's throat. He set the half-empty glass in his hand on the coffee table with a sharp clink. Drinking wouldn't help; he'd seen what it had done to his father.

Sorrel's several well-publicised affairs—not to mention one definite engagement and a possible marriage—would have tarnished that innocence. The break-up of her engagement had been splashed across newspapers and magazines, the discarded lover blurting his pain to whoever would listen. Hailed as the singer/songwriter of the decade, he'd then used his heartbreak to produce his next album—the best he'd ever done, critics had raved.

Luke didn't give a damn about the man's songs, the broken engagement, or Sorrel's love life. He had accounts to check and businesses to see to.

Scooping up the magazine with its sexy, provocative advertisement, he carried it out of the room.

He'd almost reached the office when his housekeeper emerged from the kitchen, smiling, a little cautious. 'I'm off,' she said, her glance dropping for a puzzled moment to the magazine in his hand.

'Goodnight.' He nodded without breaking his stride, and closed the office door behind him with a decisive click before firing the magazine into the rubbish bin.

He had no idea why he'd kept it. Wilful stupidity, and an itch he'd refused to scratch once and wasn't going anywhere near again.

At fifteen, the day his young, greedy stepmother had tried to seduce him, he'd vowed he wasn't going to be like his father, letting a beautiful face and tantalising body rip his heart out. No woman was ever going to acquire that much power over him.

His father's early death, followed by the discovery

of a will he'd been seduced into making during one of
his drunken bouts of self-pity, had reinforced Luke's
determination to keep that vow.

Luke considered himself a normal man with normal
needs, needs he'd never had any problem satisfying.
He'd sometimes been smugly sure of himself, he admitted, remembering a lover who'd complained that so
much charm was indecent and unfair. He'd kissed her
out of her sulks, but he knew the worth of his power,
and he exerted it with all the skill and subtlety he could
command. Although he enjoyed women, finding intense pleasure in their sleek bodies, he'd never let one
get under his skin.

Especially not Sorrel, who'd spent every school holiday at Parenga after he'd sold the house to her godmother. Very tall, and with the gangly awkwardness of
a young filly, she'd been a bashful presence on the edge
of his life, inconspicuous except for a startling swathe
of chestnut hair and those huge, innocent eyes. She'd
roused his inherent protectiveness and a sort of distant
affection, but most of the time he'd been too busy dealing with the aftermath of his father's early, disillu-
sioned death to notice her much.

And then, when he was twenty-five and she a few
weeks short of her eighteenth birthday, she'd arrived
for the summer holidays.

Luke bent to switch the computer on, and while it
hummed and muttered into action he frowned at the
screen. Somehow the schoolgirl Sorrel had metamorphosed into a serenely graceful creature, all clean lines
and shy sweetness, with an unstudied allure more exciting than anything he'd ever experienced.

Later Luke had discovered that as a Christmas gift
Cynthia had paid for a modelling course. At the time

he'd taken one stunned look at her and that smug confidence in his ability to withstand any woman had splintered, replaced by an onslaught of primitive hunger that had eaten through his self-possession with taunting ease.

For the first time he'd understood what had persuaded his father to make two disastrous marriages.

Lips compressed in a stony face, he looked around his office. Things were different now—he was no longer the young man who'd been so cockily sure of himself, and she was certainly nothing like the lovely kid who'd blushed every time she set eyes on him.

'So who cares if Sorrel Maitland is coming back?' he said aloud, his voice harsh in the silent room.

He sat down at the computer desk and called up a file, long fingers drumming impatiently on the desktop. Sometimes he wondered whether he'd have reacted so violently to Sorrel if he hadn't been caught up in a vicious legal battle with a woman who'd borne a superficial resemblance to the much younger girl.

Furious when he'd contemptuously rejected her, his stepmother had done her best to cheat him out of Waimanu, his only inheritance from his father—unless you counted the lesson that love led to pain and despair. It had taken expensive lawyers and a court case to force her to accept defeat, and it had cost Luke a vast amount of money—money he'd needed to get Waimanu on its feet again.

Yet, in spite of that, over the four weeks of that long-ago summer he'd ignored every instinct, every mental warning. In the end neither his strength of will nor his coldly incisive brain had been able to save him from losing control. He'd looked once too often into Sorrel's face, and he'd kissed her.

It still rubbed him raw to admit that he hadn't been able to stop himself. Without even trying, with no sensual invitation, no conscious temptation, the girl had had the power to shatter his will-power and the control that had become second nature.

And, once done, there had been no going back. One kiss, and he'd already been in too deep to trust himself. He'd lifted his head and gazed into those tilted, exotic eyes, dilating with dawning awareness, and realised with coldly deliberate pragmatism that if he didn't do something to end this he'd be yet another Hardcastle in thrall to an utterly unsuitable woman. Despising himself for his weakness, Luke had cut her ruthlessly out of his life.

And he'd been right; that demure innocence had been a lie. Her subsequent career had revealed that Sorrel was every bit as self-indulgent as his stepmother.

He stared down at the letter he'd crushed—one his secretary had left for him to sign.

One day he'd marry, but he'd choose carefully. The woman he planned to marry would be nothing like his mother and his stepmother, greedy women who'd used their sexual power to exact financial and emotional tribute.

When was Sorrel coming back?

And why?

Sorrel resisted the instinct to stamp on the brake as the corner hurtled too quickly towards her. Calling on skills long unused, she eased her foot back onto the accelerator to steer the unfamiliar station wagon around the corner.

'Country roads, city driver,' she said mockingly, and peered through the streaming windscreen. The wipers were doing their best, but nothing could cope with this downpour, and the falling dusk wasn't helping.

Shaking the mane of red-brown hair back from her face, she relaxed her hands on the wheel. She'd learned to drive on this road, and Luke had taught her well.

In a cowardly way she almost welcomed the strain of navigating New Zealand's northern peninsula through a wild early-summer storm. Concentration took the edge off a deeper tension—one that screwed her nerves tighter and tighter as she approached Waimanu, the huge cattle station that had been home to the proud dynasty of Hardcastles for over a century and a half.

'It's been ten years, for heaven's sake,' she muttered, frowning into the lashing rain. 'He's probably forgotten you.'

A sardonic smile tugging at her mouth, she man-oeuvred the vehicle around the final corner. Her breath hissed through her teeth when at last she eased onto the two-kilometre straight that marked the end of the road.

Where was Luke now? 'It doesn't matter,' she muttered. 'Just so long as he isn't here.'

He wouldn't be. Cynthia had told her he spent most of his time away from Waimanu. 'Making his fortune,' she'd said, sighing. 'He works far too hard, but you have to admire him. He's already got Waimanu back onto its feet, and he's branching out into corporate farming—not just here, either, but in Australia and other places. He'll be a very rich man very soon.'

Even at fourteen Sorrel had been woman enough to recognise Luke's formidable determination and the steely intelligence that controlled his tough ambition.

Physically he was immensely impressive. At six foot four, broad-shouldered and lean-hipped, he'd generated enough raw power to drive the North Island. Sorrel's mouth twisted wryly. All that and a face like a fallen angel.

And he'd been five inches taller than she was! No wonder she'd developed a massive crush on him. He'd represented dangerous masculinity, a darkly dominant force that had prowled through her unsophisticated dreams, scaring and thrilling her equally.

A scatter of hailstones across the windscreen shocked her out of her memories. She switched the lights to full; hidden somewhere in the tunnel of trees ahead was the abrupt entrance to Cynthia's house. Her house now, and her home for the next six months.

Why had Cynthia made that condition in her will? There would have been a good reason—her godmother hadn't been one for whims—but Sorrel would never know it now.

Tears clogging her lashes, she squinted into the shadows beneath the great pohutukawas that linked rugged branches above the car. Hundreds of years old, staunch survivors from their hoary crowns to the wiry aerial roots that hung down like alien nets, the trees warmed Sorrel's heart. Even without Cynthia to welcome her, this still felt like coming home—the only home she'd ever really had.

Halfway along the straight, her headlights caught a flash of light—the reflectors at Parenga's gateway. Sorrel slowed to ease the car between two stone pillars and then over the little bridge—

'Oh, *no*!'

This time her foot hit the brake pedal hard, forcing the vehicle to skid to a halt with its rear blocking the narrow road.

Sorrel stared at the ominous, fast-flowing sheet of

thick brown water pouring across the bridge. How deep did floodwater have to be before it could wash away a vehicle?

'Not very,' she said aloud, hands clenched on the wheel.

Surely the car could cope? On the far side, beyond the massed plantings of cherry trees that had been Cynthia's joy each spring, the roof of the house beckoned.

'I should be able to get through this,' Sorrel muttered on a released breath, remembering television commercials where vehicles churned their way through rivers and streams. But her car was a middle-aged station wagon, and what if a surge came downstream when she was halfway across?

A short blast from a horn whipped her head around as every misgiving about this venture roared back to life. Heart thumping in her ears, she closed her eyes for a second; when she opened them again the rain had snapped off.

She knew who was behind the wheel of the muddy Land Rover a few inches from her rear bumper.

I'm not ready! she thought. Insides knotting in an intolerable, unexpected tangle of panic, apprehension and sharp excitement, she watched Luke Hardcastle get out.

He strode towards her like some grim god of the storm—sable head held high, striking, hard-featured face set in a mask of uncompromising authority that didn't alter by the quiver of a muscle when he bent to look at her.

Sorrel swallowed quickly to ease a dry mouth and throat and unclenched her hands, only to find they were trembling so much she had to leave them tensely looped around the rim of the steering wheel.

Black brows snapping together, Luke gestured for her to open the window. She fumbled for the handle, eventually finding it.

'You can't go across,' he said curtly before the glass was fully down. 'It's not safe. Back out and drive along to the homestead.'

Sorrel moistened dry lips. 'The homestead? This *is* the homestead.'

Luke directed a pointed smile her way. 'Not any more. I've built a new one at the end of the road.' And when she still stared into his icy grey eyes he said caustically, 'I didn't plan to live in that caravan all my life, Sorrel.'

'Well—no, of course not.' Think of something sensible to say, she instructed her brain. 'Surely I can take the car across? It doesn't look very deep, and I can see where the edges of the bridge are.'

'It's too dangerous—the water's more than halfway up the wheels. Get going. This weather's unpredictable and there'll be more rain any minute,' he ordered, straightening up. 'I'll follow you.'

'Hang on—'

But he'd already turned and was heading back to his own vehicle. Despite her irritation at his arrogant air of command, Sorrel's eyes feasted on his tall figure with its long, easy stride. How often had she watched him like this—so absorbed in him that nothing else mattered?

Hundreds of times, she thought sardonically. But she'd grown out of her adolescent obsession, although it was infuriating to discover her mind hadn't yet communicated this to her body.

She wasn't afraid of giving herself away. The iron control she'd acquired while modelling clothes for autocratic photographers had been reinforced by the past two years of caring for her father.

Not that she regretted either modelling or nursing her father. Once she'd realised he missed her enough to stop eating whenever she was away on a shoot, she'd given up work, rented a house, and settled down to be his constant companion. And somehow, in the ruins of his life, they'd forged a deeper love that went beyond words.

By the time he'd died almost all of the money she'd earned from the Founiere campaign had been used in his care. It didn't matter; she'd do the same again if she had the chance.

She put the car into gear, ready to back out. Alarming though this wild song in her blood was, it had nothing to do with emotions. For some reason her body wanted Luke Hardcastle. It always had; it still did. But, although he stirred her sexually, she could control her response to his dark magnetism. Time had worked its magic healing, and she no longer thought she was in love with him.

'It's inconvenient,' she told herself firmly, 'but not disastrous.'

From behind she heard the thud of a door, followed by the sound of a thousand needles of rain on the roof as the skies opened again—almost as though the deluge had waited for Luke to get under cover.

Perhaps he really is a rain god, she thought half hysterically, wincing when headlights in the rear-vision mirror dazzled her, his swift, instantly cut signal to get a move on.

Stomach churning, she flicked her own lights to tell

him she understood and began to reverse out onto the road.

Across the bridge, two glowing eyes reflected back at her. She stamped on the brakes and switched the beam to high again.

On the far bank, and precariously perched in the branches of a half-submerged cherry tree, a large, rain-drenched cat opened its mouth wide and yowled.

'Baggie!' Sorrel fought with the door handle. Surely he hadn't been living rough since Cynthia's death? Jerking the handle, she heaved against the door, almost falling out when it swung open.

She recovered her balance and slammed the door before racing onto the bridge. Ignoring Luke's shout, and the water tearing at her legs, she focused on the cat her godmother had cherished.

'Sorrel, stop!'

Luke's roar shocked her to a halt. And once she stopped moving she could no longer stay upright. Fast and deep, the water yanked ruthlessly at her legs and feet, surging up past her knees. Terror clawed at her as she staggered, arms flailing, and began to fall.

From behind, two hard hands seized her shoulders, supporting her in a grip of steel while Luke positioned himself upstream and pushed her forward.

'Keep *moving*, damn you!' he snarled, half-hauling her with him towards the other side.

The water was building up fast, and, big man though he was, and superbly fit, Luke too had difficulty staying on his feet against its terrifying force. Something large and hidden struck the bridge, its impact driving up through the soles of Sorrel's sodden shoes.

'I'm moving, I'm moving,' she muttered, exerting

every ounce of strength to take the final few steps with him.

Once on land, he yanked her out of the silty red floodwater, strong arms imprisoning her against him. Low and lethal, his voice reverberated through her. 'You crazy idiot! What the hell's the matter with you?'

Sorrel jumped as a branch thudded into the decking.

For a paralysing second Luke's powerful body tensed against her. And in spite of the rain, heat burned through their damp clothes, lighting forbidden fires— fires instantly doused by Luke's savage voice as he pulled her several more steps back from the brink.

'If that branch had been any bigger it would have caught you—presuming you'd still been on your feet, that is.' He released her abruptly.

She shivered, remembering the way the water had sucked at her legs. 'I was making it until you yelled!'

'Not for long. What the hell were you were doing?' Luke demanded.

'Baggie's stuck in a tree.' She pointed urgently towards the cat, no longer yowling but still ominously close to the water. 'Luke, I couldn't let him drown.'

'That cat is more trouble than any other animal in the district,' he ground out. 'He's perfectly capable of looking after himself.'

'He's stuck,' Sorrel said indignantly. 'He'll fall in the water if I don't get him down.'

By then the rain had soaked them both and was beginning to seep with nasty persistence down the back of her neck.

Even dripping wet, Luke knew how to intimidate. His grey eyes glittered with sharp blue fire. Speaking with biting authority, he said, 'You're not going anywhere near that tree. The water's already around its trunk. All Baggie has to do is jump from that branch to one in the tree behind, and then he'll be able to reach solid ground.' He looked up quickly as another thud announced the arrival of more debris. 'Get into the house,' he commanded in a voice that revealed how close he was to losing his temper.

He groped in his pocket and dragged out a key ring. Tossing it to her, he said, 'The big old-fashioned one opens the back door. Now go!'

She met his uncompromising gaze with determination and a hint of defiance. 'After I've got Baggie. It's all right—I know he scratches. I'll be careful.'

'Why the sudden interest in the cat?'

Sorrel's chin jerked upwards as he scanned her face with narrow-eyed antagonism. 'He's Cynthia's cat!'

'Your godmother's been dead two years,' he said caustically, boldly chiselled features clamping into contemptuous distaste. 'I haven't noticed much concern for the damned animal in all that time.'

Flinching, she shot back, 'How would you know? You don't live here any more.'

And could have bitten out her tongue.

He gave her a lethal, narrow-eyed stare. 'Who told you that?'

'Cynthia,' she snapped. 'She said you were more or less permanently living in Auckland.'

With Mari O'Neill. Or was she at Waimanu too, now? Had they married? For a horrifying second Sorrel fought the exhausted urge to sit down and bawl her eyes out.

'I live here,' Luke told her flatly, 'at Waimanu.' Where I belong, his tone indicated, and where you are an outsider.

If she'd known that, would she have returned to Parenga?

Yes; she had nowhere else to go.

Apparently tired of this, he turned away, saying, 'I'll get the cat.'

To reach Baggie he'd have to walk out into the flood-waters. 'No!' Sorrel said swiftly, adding, 'I'll get him—he's my responsibility now.'

'Don't be ridiculous. I'm not going to stand here and watch you drown,' Luke said on a scornful note, and set off.

Sorrel's heart rocketed into overdrive when she noticed another branch twisting down the creek, its splintered branches jagged and sharp. 'Watch out!' she yelled.

He avoided it with a combination of balance, strength and lethal grace that scrambled every brain cell she possessed.

She bit onto her lower lip, only relaxing when she saw him reach the tree. As he stretched a long arm to pluck the cat from the branch, Baggie rose and with offended dignity prepared to swarm across onto the branch Luke had pointed out, from which it was a small leap to safety.

Luke grabbed him, not flinching when the cat swiped an efficient claw across his hand. Only then, honour satisfied, did Baggie settle into his arms.

When they arrived back to safety she mumbled, 'Thank you. Only—don't ever do it again, all right? I'm sorry. I really thought he was in danger.'

'In danger of pushing his luck too far,' Luke stated, putting the cat onto the ground.

'I'll take him—'

'Sorrel,' he said, his level voice more intimidating than any other man's snarled threats, 'get into the house before I lose my few remaining shreds of patience. Incredible though it might seem, I've got better things to do than stand in the rain and admire your elegant, expensively maintained body in painstaking detail.'

This time the contempt was open and forceful. She looked down, colour stinging her skin when she saw the outline of her small pointed breasts through the thin wool of her shirt.

Furious with him for being so explicit, and herself for responding so obviously, she returned scathingly, 'And I'm equally pleased to see you again, dear Luke, after all these years.'

As a retort it lost much of its effect in a shiver that tumbled the words through her teeth.

His laughter was low and humourless, as cold as the ice-grey eyes that raked her face. 'Sorry, I'm all out of warm welcomes. Get going before you develop hypothermia!'

Pulses racing in the aftermath of adrenalin overload, she turned and ran up the drive to the back door, not caring whether he followed her or stayed out in the rain.

The key turned and the door yielded to her wet hand. In the big mud-room she switched on the light, watching as Luke rummaged in a cupboard and produced an old towel with which he proceeded to give Baggie a quick, effective rubdown.

Sorrel hovered, resenting the way the light picked out the tanned skin drawn over the strong, thrusting bone structure that would make him a striking man all his life. Her stomach performed a flip, and she began to shiver. No, she thought desperately. Not now—not ever again! Not Luke.

He looked up, guarded eyes forbidding as the iron-blue gleam on a sword blade. 'Welcome back,' he drawled.

CHAPTER TWO

Sorrel blurted, 'We're stuck here, aren't we? It's too dangerous to go back over the bridge.'

'True,' Luke answered, the single derisive word setting her teeth on edge.

Marooned with the last man in the world she'd choose! And her clothes and make-up—horrors, even her toothbrush!—as inaccessible as the far side of the moon.

Flushing, she said between her teeth, 'I sent a box out from America—'

'It arrived a week ago—I put it in your bedroom.'

'Thanks.' So she had clothes. She hastily wrenched her gaze from Luke's soaked torso and broad shoulders. 'You can't stay like that without getting pneumonia or rheumatism or something.'

'We'll have to improvise,' he said coolly. 'When the box arrived I deduced you'd be following it, so I rang the power authority and Telecom, only to find you'd already arranged for the utilities to be switched on. A hot shower will ward off hypothermia, which is much more likely than either pneumonia or rheumatism.'

He stooped to put a wriggling Baggie onto the floor. Sorrel's mouth dried as she noted the smooth play of muscles beneath his shirt.

Indignation burned through her. She'd been so sure she was over Luke. Darn it, sometimes she went for a week at a time without thinking of him. And it hadn't ever been anything more than a crush—and one searing

kiss. Now the years she'd spent away from Parenga
might just as well not have happened! One glance into
his grey eyes and she'd reverted straight back to pa-
thetic adolescence.

It could stop right there. Falling in lust with Luke
would be taking a direct route to misery. He seemed to
despise her, and she—well, she was going to guard her
heart too well for him to break it again.

Yawning, Baggie stretched voluptuously and, with a
controlled self-possession that reminded Sorrel of the
other male in the room, paced across to a bowl and
looked up with regal expectancy. The cat's damp black
fur stuck to a sturdy, far-from-starving body. Either
someone had been looking after him or he was more
than capable of fending for himself.

Sorrel could hear the reluctance in her husky voice
as she said, 'There are towels in the box. I'm sorry,
Luke. Dashing across to rescue Baggie was foolish of
me.'

'Extremely,' he told her with brutal honesty. 'No animal is worth risking your life for.'

Pitched back into adolescence again, she demanded,
'What about the horse you saved from a cyclone one
Christmas holiday? You *swam* across the river to bring
it back. At least I had a bridge under my feet!'

He shrugged. 'I was young and stupid. Besides, the
horse would have died. Baggie was perfectly safe. He's
a con artist and saw a chance to get a ride back to
Waimanu without getting his feet wet.'

She parried his sardonic survey with her most aloof
expression. 'It was just the shock of seeing him.
After—when Cynthia died I organised the vet to come
and collect him. They told me he'd been taken in by a
friend, and then—well, I was busy...' Busy fulfilling

her contract for the wretched Founiere campaign, busy caring for her father.

She bit her lip. 'I just assumed Baggie was safe. I had no idea *you* were looking after him.'

Luke looked at her dispassionately. Even soaking wet and bedraggled, her rare, intoxicating beauty blazed forth, intensified now by an aura of controlled, poised sensuality. Savagely dismissing the image of her in another man's arms, he decided that she'd been a hugely successful model because she appealed to men's secret fantasies and women's insecurities.

'I told the vet to leave him here,' he said abrasively. 'Why didn't you ask me if I'd take care of him? You didn't need to have him put down—'

'Put down?' Long lashes shot up to reveal darkening gold-centred eyes as she stared accusingly at him. 'Who said anything about putting him down?'

She did it very well, he thought cynically—all outrage and hurt feelings. 'That's what the vet thought you wanted him to do.'

Almost she bared her teeth at him. 'I did not! They misunderstood. I wanted him safe in the vet clinic cattery, not living rough.' Gracefully she stooped to stroke the animal, her wet clothes moulding the feminine curves of her hips and breasts.

Luke cursed silently as his body began to harden.

But although he couldn't control this consuming, primitive response, he could certainly ignore it. Noting her shiver when she straightened up, he commanded curtly, 'Get upstairs and under a shower.'

'But what about you?'

'I'll shower in the downstairs bathroom.' When she didn't move he ran his gaze over her and asked in a soft, deliberately taunting voice, 'Do you need help to take off your clothes?'

It worked.

Sorrel stiffened. 'No!'

Halfway up the stairs she realised that he'd known exactly how she'd react. All right, she thought, setting her jaw; round one to Luke.

But this wasn't going to be a battle. Because she had to stay at Parenga for six months to fulfil Cynthia's wishes, and, as Luke was apparently living right next door, she'd have to establish a friendly relationship with him.

Friendly? an interested voice inside her head asked smoothly.

Yes, friendly! she snarled back. If she decided to set up Parenga as an exclusive bed and breakfast, she couldn't afford to antagonise Luke. Not only did he have a lot of clout in Northland, but as her closest neighbour he'd have input into the District Council's deliberations.

Leaning over the balustrade, she called, 'I'll open the box and bring down some towels.'

'OK.'

She ran up the rest of the stairs and pushed open the door of her old bedroom. Although the box had already been opened, a glance revealed that the contents were still sealed. Luke, no doubt. He thought of everything.

Slow rigors moved through her while she scrabbled through its contents. They didn't seem much to represent ten years of her life, yet this was all she'd salvaged—a few clothes, some soft goods, and the clothes in the car.

Sorrel sat back on her haunches and stared across the room; a rising wind was hurling vicious bullets of rain at the window, recalling the rain on the other side of the world when she'd packed the box after her father's death. She'd been weeping, and the house in which her father had died after a two years of misery had sighed heavily as it settled around her.

Yet, grief-stricken as she was, she felt only gratitude for his death; he had longed for it passionately since the day he'd been struck down.

Her shaking fingers found the towels; she got up and carried them out of the bedroom, stopping a few paces from the doorway when she saw Luke halfway up the stairs.

'There you go,' she said, handing the huge green bath sheets over to him. 'No soap, I'm afraid.'

She felt his regard, noted the way he paused a fraction of a second before answering, 'Thank you. You're starting to go pale. Get under the shower.'

He, of course, was entirely unaffected by his dousing!

Once in the bathroom Sorrel fumbled with the buttons of her shirt, her cold fingers making it difficult. By the time she got it off the shivers had turned to shaking; she had to clench her teeth as she unzipped her trousers, stepped out of them and turned on the shower.

She could cope with living next door to Luke. She had to. She had nowhere else to go and no other assets than Parenga.

'All you need to do is stay cool and make sure you don't fall in lust with him,' she said on a faint, humourless smile.

Blocking the memories, she let the water play over her sensitised body.

* * *

As Sorrel was coming back down, barefoot but warm again, in jeans and a long, loose shirt unearthed from the box, she heard the door to the laundry open and close. Relief whispered through her. Of course, the drier was functional, which meant Luke could dry his clothes. Like the stove and the washing machine and the fridge, the drier was part of the leased chattels.

She'd spent her time under the shower using calming techniques she'd mastered during the past years. As always, they had centred her and soothed her, so she really thought she was ready for Luke.

But when she saw him coming along the passage, naked except for the bath sheet wrapped around his lean hips and muscular thighs, her carefully manufactured composure evaporated, ambushed by a barrage of sensation that dried her mouth and electrified every cell in her body.

Only born Scottish Highlanders got away with wearing a skirt, and even they had to call them kilts and jazz them up with pleats and tartans and phallic daggers, not to mention well-cut jackets and snow-white shirts.

Luke did *not* look ridiculous. The moss-green towel contrasting superbly with his coppery hide, he strode towards her, a dark, dangerous male from every woman's most primal dreams, sleek and lethal, grey gaze hooded. The only time he'd kissed her she'd seen electric blue lightning in his eyes, but now they were as burnished and opaque as old silver.

Throat tight, Sorrel surged into speech. 'How long do you think it will take the creek to go down?' she asked, holding his gaze with hers in an attempt to block out the impact of burnished skin over coiled muscles.

'When the tide goes out,' he said evenly. 'Probably

in the early hours of the morning. But if this rain keeps on it might not happen even then. I'll have to stay here.'

Spend the night alone with Luke? A man who looked like something hot-blooded and barbaric from a dim and romantic past? Sorrel's bare toes curled onto the carpet and in the pit of her stomach a forbidden rhythm began to drum, slow and deep and sensual.

'Why on earth was this house built here?' She knew she sounded petulant, but kept doggedly on. 'Between the creek and the estuary, for heaven's sake! Even though your ancestors relied on sea access, surely they must have considered the possibility of the creek flooding.'

His brows rose as he said with infuriating patience, 'Why should they? Scows used to come up the river—which was much deeper then—to the wharf below the house. And they were careful to build on a rise that didn't flood.'

'Just as well,' she said lamely. She fixed her eyes on a point just beyond one bare, broad shoulder, and said brightly, 'I wonder what Baggie's cat food tastes like—is there any here, or do you feed him at Waimanu?'

His mouth curved. 'You won't have to steal from him. When I found out you were coming I organised some staples.'

'Staples?' she echoed, eyelashes flickering as she resisted the urge to retreat. Get a grip, she told herself scornfully; you're behaving like a half-wit! Or a kid who's so deep in a crush she can only think with her hormones.

Laconically he told her, 'Flour, tinned stuff, a few plates and some cutlery, pots and pans—my housekeeper worked out what you might need. It's in the pantry, and there's food in the deep freeze too.'

'Thank you very much.' Stiffening her spine, she turned and walked ahead of him into the kitchen. 'It's very kind of you. You must tell me how much I owe you.'

There was a moment of silence before he drawled, 'It seemed a neighbourly thing to do. I'll send you a bill.'

He was offended? Well, so was she; clearly he thought her too dim-witted to have brought cutlery or crockery, not to mention food, and too thick to think of organising the power and telephone. In the car was a large container of just such staples as he'd mentioned, as well as fresh food in a chilly-bin.

On the other hand, it was she who'd landed them in this ridiculous situation.

She opened the pantry door and stared blindly at an array of tinned and packaged foods, trying to put out of her treacherous mind the image of Luke, big and bronzed and gleaming behind her, clad in nothing but a towel.

Aloud she said, 'On a night like this a casserole would be perfect, but soup will be simpler.' The lights flickered ominously. Ignoring Luke's muttered expletive, she added, 'And faster. I hope the storm doesn't bring down the power lines.'

'Can you make soup?' He didn't try to hide his scepticism.

Sorrel was rather proud of the steady voice in which she said, 'Yes. Is there any firewood in the lean-to? I wish I'd thought to get one of the heaters out of storage, but I was intent on getting home.'

'Home?' he said, without inflection.

'Parenga's always seemed like home.' Sorrel reached for a packet, clutching it as she pretended to study the label. 'I'll put some soup on.'

'I'll see if there's any firewood in the lean-to. Call if you need help,' he said insufferably.

She waited until she heard the door close behind him before letting out an explosive breath.

Call if she needed help? Not bloody likely. She wouldn't give him the satisfaction. And she'd make him literally eat his doubts about her cooking prowess.

Half an hour later, after several other ominous electrical fluctuations, she carried a mug and a bowl of soup into the bookroom—empty of furniture, like the rest of the house. When Cynthia's death had been followed almost immediately by her father's stroke, Sorrel had been forced to store her godmother's furniture and pay an agency to let the house.

It wasn't the forlorn bookroom, shelves empty of books, denuded of everything but heavy drapes and carpet, that stole her breath and set her nerves vibrating.

Luke was leaning forward to dump another couple of logs onto the fire in the hearth. Light gleamed in slabs of copper and rose and gold over his torso, and struck flames from his dark hair. He looked all forbidden male, big and competent and compelling.

And sexy as hell.

A few feet away Baggie sat with tail curled around his paws, surveying both man and fire with benign satisfaction.

Sorrel ventured further into the room, trying to conceal her disturbing response to so much unadulterated masculinity. As well as his potent physical attributes, Luke's tough, hard-edged face was handsome enough to catch any woman's eye, but it was the bone-deep

charisma radiating from him, an exciting combination
of power and authority and a mesmerising sexual
charge, that demolished her carefully built defences.

A long-repressed hunger exploded into life.

Ignoring it, she said chattily, 'I'd forgotten how
chilly it could get in a summer storm.' With her heart
thudding erratically in her chest, she offered Luke the
bowl of soup.

He accepted it, brows lifting cynically when she
made sure their fingers didn't touch. 'Smells superb.
Here, give me that mug before you sit down.'

'I'll just get the toast.' Putting the mug on the floor,
she escaped, to breathe deeply all the way to the
kitchen and back.

Once seated in front of the fire, toast-rack between
them like a small fence, Sorrel kept her gaze fixed on
her mug, hoping Luke didn't realise how conscious she
was of his nakedness beneath the towel.

'The soup's excellent,' he said laconically.

As far as eating his words went it didn't go far
enough, but it was clearly all she was going to get. She
said with dulcet irony, 'It's amazing what you can do
with a few tins and some dried herbs.'

Without tasting it she drank some, then hugged the
mug with her hands, as forlorn and useless a shield as
the toast-rack. 'Tomorrow I'll go into Kerikeri and sort
out the furniture.' It cost money she could ill afford to
keep in storage.

'If the road's open,' he said negligently.

Sorrel stiffened. 'Is it likely to close?'

'It looked as though it could slip at the top of the
hill.'

Of course it was no big deal to him, but if it did the
power would inevitably go off. Sorrel brooded over the

likelihood of being forced to camp at Parenga until it
was restored, but soon thrust the thought away. She
couldn't do anything about it now.

The scent of the soup, rich and savoury, mingled
with that of the toast, and the eucalyptus logs on the
fire. Sorrel drank more of hers before saying lightly, 'Is
Baggie still obsessive about hunting eels?'

She smiled at the cat, amused to see him yawn elab-
orately, tongue flicking over his sharp teeth as though
reminiscing about past successes.

Luke gave a quick grin. 'Yes, although he and the
eels periodically have a slight difference of opinion
over who is catching whom.'

'Cynthia used to hope he'd grow out of it.'

'That's the problem with obsessions—they're not
easy to overcome.' His voice altered. 'Where's your
husband?'

'*What?*' She looked up to meet coldly metallic eyes.
'Is this some kind of joke? I don't have a husband.'

He watched her steadily. 'When you dropped out of
sight a couple of years ago there were hints that you
had married.'

'*I dropped out* to look after my father.' After a pause
she finished steadily, 'He had a stroke.'

'How is he now?'

She got to her feet and walked across to the window.
While she'd been showering the quick New Zealand
darkness had fallen, and all she could see now were the
pink goblets of a magnolia tossing wildly in the wind
and the rain.

'He's dead,' she said bleakly. 'He died a month ago.
I've just taken him… He's buried beside my mother.'

'I'm sorry.' Luke's voice was guarded.

Sorrel turned away from the destruction outside to

pin a small, lopsided smile onto her lips. 'Actually it was a relief for him. He spent those two years being lifted from a bed to a wheelchair, and he hated it. He couldn't even speak. We developed a sort of code with eyelash blinks, but after a while he just tried very hard to die.'

Once he'd managed to communicate his bitter regret for everything he'd done and ask her forgiveness he'd given up, unable to bear the burden of what he saw as his betrayal and the subsequent ruin of her life.

'Hell,' Luke said, getting lithely to his feet and coming across to stand in front of her.

To her astonishment he took her cold hands in his lean, callused ones and held them until they began to warm up. The uncompromising lines of his face had softened, and she read real concern in his dark eyes.

Sorrel blinked back tears. 'Quite literally hell for him. He was desperately unhappy.'

'Did you nurse him?'

Because it was too poignant to stand there with him, she gave a little tug of her captive hands. He released them and stood back to let her sit down again. Crossing her legs, she stared into the fire, mug of soup clutched firmly. 'With help.'

Luke reached out a long arm and snagged another log from the box beside the fire. From beneath lowered eyelids Sorrel watched the towel slide a little way down his flexing hips. Luke turned and caught her, his eyes narrowing into icy grey slivers.

Without any embarrassment he hitched up the towel. 'What made you decide to come back to Parenga?'

'I love it here,' she told him.

'Pull the other leg.' Raindrops hit the windows in a violent blast as he probed silkily, 'What's the real reason?' When she didn't answer, his voice hardened. 'I want the truth, Sorrel.'

Her eyes turned opaque, her gloriously sensuous mouth tightening for less than a second before relaxing into a smile that was a secretive taunt, infinitely alluring, coolly self-possessed.

Dropping her voice a few notes, she said, 'You're an arrogant—' She bit back the first word that came to mind, and with a sweet smile substituted, '*man*, Luke. What makes you think you can demand answers from me?'

His stomach muscles contracted as though she'd hit him in the solar plexus. Much as he'd like to, he couldn't counter her direct challenge by shaking the truth out of her. 'How long will you be here?'

Sorrel's lashes drooped. 'For the next six months, anyway.'

'Doing what?'

'Whatever I want to.' She fixed him with an enigmatic gaze, her lips curving into another of the slow-burning incitements to riot that had scorched out from thousands of photographs—fire beneath ice, control heated by passion's subtle, elemental lure. 'Don't worry, I plan to stick close to home. You won't even know I'm here.'

Going purely on instinct, he said, 'Sell Parenga back to me. Get a couple of land agents to value it; I'll pay a fair price.'

'What would you do with it?'

'I'd find something.'

He was too good a negotiator to watch her closely, but he'd have learned nothing from her guarded expression. She was, of course, a professional at assuming a mask.

'I can't sell it,' she said with composure. 'Cynthia left it to me in a trust.'

'That must have been a shock.' His eyes narrowed when she hesitated and turned her head, her profile etched against to the flames, elegant from the high forehead to the winged brows and short straight nose. *Elegant*, however, was not the term he'd use to describe her sultry mouth—or that surprisingly determined chin.

'Why?' she asked with a delicate flick of astonishment. 'The only thing that saved Waimanu for you was the family trust your father set up.'

Luke's mouth twisted. True. His stepmother hadn't been able to overturn the trust. But she'd spent enough money in the legal battle to almost bleed the station dry.

He said, 'So who was Cynthia protecting Parenga from?'

Another shrug, another cool dismissal from Sorrel's magnificent eyes, wide and challenging as a cat's. 'Nobody. She was a careful woman, I suppose. Or perhaps your experience frightened her.'

The fire hissed, sending up a shaft of blue-green flame that illuminated her flawless ivory skin—skin that attracted touch with its translucence.

Hunger ate into Luke's gut. Cursing it, he told himself he didn't care what she did. In spite of that potent sexual magnetism she meant nothing to him. But something was going on here that he didn't understand. It drove him to ask deliberately, 'She didn't say?'

'No.' But he suspected from her tone that she knew.

For some reason he recalled her car: tough, a workhorse ideally suited for Northland country roads—and about seven years old. An odd vehicle for a successful model.

Sorrel held out her hand to the cat, but Baggie eyed her inscrutably, ignoring the graceful beckoning fingers.

Luke watched her hand fall onto the carpet. Stop this, instinct told him. You don't want to know anything about her—she's dangerous.

But he said curtly, 'Are you hiding?'

'No.'

Her voice was almost amused. If he hadn't seen the momentary tension of her facial muscles he might almost have believed her.

To hide a quick, inconvenient surge of protectiveness, he said curtly, 'You can tell me if you're in trouble.'

She hesitated, her eyes evading his, then laughed, an artificial little sound that reminded him unpleasantly of his stepmother.

'I'm not in any trouble, and I have no ulterior reason for coming to Parenga. I just want to regroup—think things through. Why do you find that so surprising?'

'I'd have thought you'd go back to the world you've made your own.'

Her spine stiffened. 'Two years is a long time, and the fashionable world has a short memory.'

He watched with sardonic interest as her lashes slipped down to hide her wide eyes. She produced another slow smile that lingered enticingly on her soft, full mouth. He'd seen his stepmother do exactly that—use the promise of sex to get what she wanted.

But he'd never before felt anything like this ferocious surge of lust.

Despising himself for his weakness, he reminded himself that although Sorrel had left Waimanu a lovely innocent it hadn't taken her long to collect her first scalp, and there'd been a procession after that.

OK, so much of the gossip was probably fabricated, but if even half of it was false she'd had a lot of men in her life—men she'd discarded without even an attempt at finesse. She'd have made enemies.

He said, 'Are you saying that you've made your pile and now you're ready to enjoy it?'

'I'm saying that at my age I'm not going to find any modelling jobs,' she snapped. 'It's over, done, kaput! I'm twenty-eight, Luke, and that's too old to start again.'

Unwilling to meet his glinting, perceptive gaze, she bent to pick up the empty mug and bowl and toast-rack and wondered what he was thinking.

Nothing good, she decided wearily after a swift glance at his uncompromising features.

He surprised her by standing up in one powerful, fluid movement. When she began to follow suit, he helped her up, his grip casual yet smoothly, effortlessly powerful.

Releasing her, he said, 'The clothes should be dry by now.'

He held open the door, standing back to let her through. The touch of his calloused hands still running like jagged fire through her, she reluctantly obeyed the unspoken order.

As she passed him Sorrel smelt the faint fragrance—a combination of soap and exciting essence of sexy male—that was Luke's alone.

Her step faltered; she was catapulted back in time and memories she'd long repressed sprang new-minted to her mind—memories of that last summer, when she'd been so desperately in love with him.

Sheer terror hollowed out her stomach. She wasn't going through that again.

'Thank you,' she said stonily.

Closing the door behind them both, Luke said, 'It's nothing.' Mockery underpinned the words.

Sorrel turned to find him far too close. Pulses jerking, she took a swift step backwards. For a moment they stared at each other; she saw flames leap up in the grey eyes and thought stupidly, *But there's no fire here in the hall.*

And then the flames died, blanked out by Luke's strong will. He scanned her face with cynical detachment.

Sorrel swivelled away and concentrated on walking steadily into the kitchen. Once there, she deposited the tray on the bench with enough force to set every piece of crockery jumping. Although she couldn't hear him over the rain, she could feel his presence on her skin, right through to her bones.

Breathe slow, breathe easy, she commanded herself as she ignored him to stack the dishes in the sink. The light flickered again while she groped for the plug and turned on the water.

From behind, Luke said dispassionately, 'I meant what I said—if you're in any trouble, I might be able to help.'

Her fingers closed around the handle of the mug. 'I'm not,' she said, giving it a vigorous slosh in the soapy water. Luke's housekeeper was a gem; she'd even remembered detergent. 'Unless you call the imminent loss of power trouble,' she finished flippantly.

This tense conversation—like the thrust and parry of a fencing match—at least stopped her from wondering where they were going to sleep that night.

Aware of Luke's darkening gaze, she spread a clean handkerchief over the draining dishes, grimacing as the wind hurled more rain against the windows.

'When you get back into your clothes,' she said tonelessly, 'you'd better put the towels in after them—we might need them to sleep on. Unless you organised that too, there are no beds, blankets or duvets.'

He said smoothly, 'Fortunately we have a fire and plenty of wood.'

The door closed quietly behind him, and after a silent moment Sorrel heard a low rumble from floor level. 'You,' she said severely as Baggie wove around her ankles, 'are a shameless and opportunistic cat. I don't know why Cynthia loved you so much. Just because I fell for that fake ''Save me, I'm going to drown'' act of yours I have to spend the night on the floor in front of the fire.'

With Luke.

Fate couldn't have thought up a more unkind trick to play.

Be fair, her rational mind coaxed. If Luke hadn't come along when he did you'd have dashed across the bridge and quite possibly drowned. As it is you're safe, and so is Luke. 'And so are you,' she said to the cause of this inconvenience. 'But then you always would have been!'

Whereas she and Luke were alone until the creek went down.

She'd been so sure that time and distance had exorcised this heated enchantment of the senses. She'd been wrong; even thinking about spending the night with Luke sent her pulse rate soaring, and the dampness in her palms was a straight regression to that painful, ecstatic first love.

It meant nothing, though. Just a kick in the blood, a synthetic addiction to something Luke possessed that no other man appeared to. None she'd met, anyway.

Another shiver of light from the lamp galvanised her into filling the electric kettle and plugging it in. There wasn't any milk, but Luke presumably still drank his coffee black.

A couple of minutes later, carrying a mug of hot coffee, she left the kitchen with Baggie. In the hall, Luke was hanging up the telephone, overwhelmingly sophisticated in a superb Italian cotton shirt and trousers that had been made for him. In fact, she was pretty sure she could give the name of his tailor—an English one.

His years of hard work had definitely paid off. And she was glad of it—he deserved it.

'I thought it was worth a try, but the phone's off, and judging by the fluctuations in the power that'll go soon,' he said briefly. 'Stupidly, I left my mobile in the Land Rover.'

'Is there anyone you need to let know?' Sorrel held her breath.

CHAPTER THREE

'NO ONE.'

Abrupt and emotionless, the word hung without resonance in the damp air. Odd, humiliating relief relaxed Sorrel's tense muscles.

Another blast of wind howled in from the sea and flung itself against the house. The lights flickered and this time, as Luke swore succinctly, they went out, stranding them in thick darkness.

'Stay where you are,' he commanded. 'Don't spill that coffee on yourself.'

He opened the door into the bookroom so that the warm glow of the fire showed her where to go. Carrying the mug carefully, she went in, putting it onto the floor before sitting cross-legged in front of the fire.

After adding another couple of logs to the flames Luke joined her, long legs stretched out on the floor.

'Here,' she said, offering the mug.

He took the mug, but instead of drinking he asked, 'Where's yours?'

'I can't sleep if I drink coffee after dinner,' she told him. 'Goodness, listen to that rain! I hope our cars are all right.'

'Don't worry about them; the creek's never risen above the road.'

The darkness outside was split open by vivid light, gone as swiftly as it came. 'I'd forgotten how heavily it rains here in summer,' she said wryly. She would have liked to close the curtains, but that would make the situation far too intimate.

'It's due to pass over tomorrow. We often get storms from the tropics at this time of year.'

He might have meant to be soothing, but Sorrel thought she discerned a note of impatience beneath his words. Tartly she said, 'I know that.'

'Did you want comforting? Sorry, I don't have much time for spoilt women.' His voice was cool and steady, delivering each word with a crisp lack of compromise that flayed her emotions. 'Or spoilt men, come to that.'

'I'm sure you don't realise how smug and judgmental you sound! My life is my business.'

'If you're going to be living next door to me it may turn out to be my business too,' he said, lifting the mug to his lips.

'It won't be,' she said shortly.

When Luke's eyes drifted to her exposed neck and then back up to her ear lobes, heat scorched her skin. She wished she'd left her hair down, and for once worn a bra.

Too loudly she told him, 'I don't throw wild parties and play loud music all night. I might cross your land to walk on the beach, but that's the only time you're likely to see me. I'll be as good a neighbour as Cynthia.'

Unexpectedly he said, 'I'm sorry I missed her funeral. I was stuck up in the Andes with a government primary industries delegation, and I didn't hear about it until I arrived back in New Zealand.'

Sorrel's teeth clamped onto her bottom lip and she looked away to hide the sheen of tears in her eyes. 'I wasn't there either,' she said in a shaky voice. 'But— she'd have understood.'

Her breath stopped in her throat as strong fingers enclosed hers, once more offering warmth and support. A glance revealed nothing in his expression but distant sympathy, but once again that unsubtle excitement charged through her like a bolt of lightning, burning away everything but her body's involuntary response.

Her brain went into meltdown, just as it had when she'd been a thin, shy teenager, acutely embarrassed by her height and dazzled by his open sexual charisma.

Don't be fooled—this is just chemistry, she told herself sturdily, a matter of pheromones and subliminal signals left over from the distant, primitive past.

She was no longer a shy virgin; this sexual thrill was wonderful, but it wasn't all that important. What mattered in a relationship was respect, and love, and shared interests and values. And she had nothing in common with Luke.

An upward glance revealed him examining her, one side of his mouth tilted in irony as he assessed her response.

Showered by ice, she muttered, 'Thanks,' and tugged her hand free.

Luke let it go, thinking mordantly that it was still there, that blatant, unwanted reaction. Looking into slumbrous green eyes, mysteriously dark in the muted fire-glow, he noticed the soft parting of her mouth.

An innate masculine instinct, honed by a fair amount of experience, told him it wouldn't be difficult to get her into bed. Beneath that restrained, exquisitely composed surface Sorrel was sending off enough signals to organise a naval exercise. Sardonically he wondered whether she was doing it deliberately.

He clamped down on a wild upwelling of hunger,

carnal and potent. Before he took what she was offering, he needed to know why she was offering it.

'I liked her enormously,' he said quietly. 'She was gallant and kind and always bright and entertaining, with a heart big enough to act as the local agony aunt. I miss her.'

Sorrel deliberately relaxed tense muscles. His expression hadn't altered even though he must have felt her pulses leap under his touch. At least the dimness would have hidden her heightened colour. It was plain he didn't feel anything like the overwhelming anticipation licking through her like a forest fire, beautiful and deadly.

But now he knew that she still wanted him.

What he must never discover was that she'd always measured men by his standards—and none of them had made the grade.

Would he laugh if he ever realised he'd stood between her and every other man she'd met?

Probably. But he wouldn't believe it.

So she raised her head and met his unsparing gaze. 'I miss her too.'

'I'm surprised. You hadn't seen much of her since you left,' he said blandly.

'I saw her at least once or twice a year,' she said defensively. 'And we talked often on the phone.'

One dark brow lifted to devastating effect. 'Did you?'

'Yes.' And although they sounded like an excuse she couldn't prevent the next sharp words. 'I don't imagine Cynthia told you everything she did.'

'She certainly didn't mention regular telephone calls,' he returned caustically.

Temper flaring, Sorrel said, 'So because she didn't

mention them you don't believe they happened? You know, you're going to have to work on this habit of judging people.'

'I haven't seen you since the day you left Waimanu to go to New York,' he returned. 'I may not have been here often, but if you'd made regular visits to Cynthia I'd have known.'

Except that whenever she'd come back she'd asked Cynthia for privacy. More thunder rolled around the sky, the rain dropping so heavily that the fire spat and crackled.

Luke said indolently, 'Tell me what it was like being a world-famous model. Did you enjoy it?'

'It had its moments. A lot of it was boring,' she said before she could stop herself. She gave a shocked little laugh and stared into the flames. 'And that's the first time I've admitted that.'

'If you didn't like it, why did you do it?'

Why indeed? 'I went to fabulous places,' she said lightly, 'and met people who were fascinating and stimulating and exciting.'

'I imagine the money would have been hard to resist,' he said sardonically.

'Money is nice. You must agree—you've worked hard enough for yours.'

Luke gave a taut smile. 'Your eyes still glitter green fire when you're angry,' he said, his gaze lingering on her mouth until she felt it softening and heating.

'Don't be patronising,' she retorted.

With forceful precision he said, 'I worked for Waimanu and for the people who earn their living from it.'

'Very noble,' Sorrel said idly.

He looked her over with unhurried deliberation. 'So

modelling didn't entirely fulfil its promise of glamour and high living? I remember a girl who couldn't wait to get away from New Zealand.'

Because he'd just started a hot and heavy affair with Mari O'Neill.

Her smile was as edged as his tone. 'Naturally. What eighteen-year-old girl would turn down an opportunity like that? And what's the difference between a woman—or man—using his or her physical attributes to earn a living, and one who uses her intelligence?'

Luke put the coffee mug down. 'Simply that using intelligence indicates hard work and effort, whereas—'

'Believe me,' she said sardonically, 'a lot of hard—very hard—work goes into maintaining those physical attributes you're so contemptuous of.'

'Contempt doesn't come into it. I'm as affected by beauty as any other person,' he said coolly.

'But you still feel that those with good brains should be applauded for using the assets they were handed in the genetic lottery, whereas those with good bodies shouldn't. I never thought you were a Puritan, Luke.'

She paused, and when he said nothing added with delicate malice, 'Or a hypocrite. Don't try to convince me that your handsome face—' she ran her gaze over it with studied insolence '—and excellent physique haven't made your life easier, even if it's only your love life.'

He astounded her by laughing softly. 'I concede your point. However, it seems a shame to waste an intelligent brain like yours.'

'Ah, but brains don't deteriorate,' she said, irritated because even accusing him of hypocrisy hadn't pricked his temper.

'What have you been doing with yours?'

Two years ago she'd taken a rapid—and very depressing—course in accounting practice, for one thing! 'Using it,' she said curtly, glad when another blast of wind hit the house. She scrambled to her feet. 'I'll pull the curtains.'

She felt Luke's eyes on her as she yanked one of the heavy drapes across the long French windows. Wildly fluttering flakes in the thickening darkness outside caught her eye. 'Oh!'

'What is it?' he asked, instantly on his feet.

'It's all right—it's just the last flowers from the magnolia.'

Torn pink shreds of the glorious chalices were being driven by the merciless wind into drifts and ridges across the brick terrace, and there battered into a mess by the rain. Shivering, Sorrel shut them out.

'Cynthia loved them so much,' she said remotely as she sat down, carefully keeping almost the full width of the fireplace between her and the man who dominated the room.

She should have left the curtains open—now the room was like a cave, disturbingly intimate, the firelight swallowed by empty corners and heavy drapes.

Exhaustion suddenly ached through her, but a rapid glance at her watch revealed that it was far too early to even think of sleeping. Thankful for the glossy mask derived from years spent producing exactly the look each photographer wanted, she gave Luke a slow, glimmering smile. 'What happened to Mari O'Neill?'

'She's taking the corporate world by storm,' he said blandly. 'What happened to that young actor you were linked with a couple of months after you left?'

'No romance—just PR for both of us,' she said with a touch of awkwardness. 'He wanted the publicity and

my agent—' and her father '—felt it would be good
for my career.'

The unromantic nature of their relationship hadn't
stopped the man from trying to seduce her, but he'd
given up with good grace when she refused him. He
was one of the few friends who'd visited her during
her father's illness.

Luke's mouth curled. 'And did it work?'

'I suppose so.' She felt as though she was fighting a
duel, using words to deflect a long-repressed pain. A
yawn took her by surprise. She covered it with her
hand, but of course he saw it.

He frowned. 'Did you fly in today?'

'Yes, from Vancouver.' She made a face. 'Normally
I never get jet-lagged, but driving up was a bit exciting.'

'City driver.' But there was a note of amusement in
the reply.

Sorrel dragged her eyes away from his darkly arrogant features. A hot urgency exploded in the pit of her
stomach. She leaned forward and looped her arms
around her knees, staring into the flames. Baggie,
curled up a few feet away, opened his eyes and
stretched, then began to purr, a pleasant domestic coun-
terpoint to the weather outside and the bewildering turmoil of her thoughts and reactions.

Feeling as though her head was stuffed with cotton
wool, Sorrel hid another yawn, but Luke saw it.

'You're worn out,' he said roughly, getting to his
feet. 'I'll make up beds while you get ready.'

Sorrel looked up with cool eyes and a tight mouth.
'If I go to sleep now I'll wake up at some ungodly hour
of the morning with my body clock still out of kilter.

It's a pity we haven't got a pack of cards—I'd take you on at poker. Or we could take turns to play patience.'

He laughed. 'I don't think it would work,' he said enigmatically.

Sorrel lifted a dismissive shoulder and turned back to rest her chin on her knees again, folding her arms tightly across her shins. The flames danced in front of her—beckoning, dangerous.

Tension warred with her debilitating tiredness. Better give in to the tiredness—yielding to temptation was becoming a seductive option. She said, 'I don't suppose you can produce a toothbrush?'

'No brush, and no toothpaste either,' he said unsparingly.

She sighed. 'There are distinct advantages to civilisation. I noticed salt in the kitchen; I'll use that.'

'I filled the bath in case the power went off, so we have that, but if you want warm water to wash your face you'd better take the jug from the kitchen.'

'I'd forgotten,' she said in a subdued voice.

'No power, no pump, no water.' Her silence must have been eloquent because he gave a soft derisive laugh. 'This is the wilds of New Zealand. You should have gone to the Seychelles or some other expensively exclusive place for your holiday.'

He hadn't *tried* to hurt her, she acknowledged as she got to her feet and made her way out of the room, obeying his injunction to leave the door open behind her. But the casual jibe stung.

Halfway through finger-brushing her teeth, she heard a movement outside the bathroom. 'I'll be out in a minute,' she called.

'I'm going up to bring that box of clothes down.'

She rinsed her mouth. 'The box is too big—just grab as many clothes as you can. I'll come up—'

'Stay where you are. It's damned dark here.'

In the heavy darkness she strained to hear his sure-footed progress. To be home with Luke had once been her sole ambition—the hoped-for, yearned-for haven of the heart. She'd never had it.

But she was over that, thank heavens.

So how did she feel about him now?

Wary, she decided, groping her way back to the bookroom. Very wary. The years had changed him in subtle ways she didn't understand. She sensed a hard authority that hadn't been evident before.

And the swift stab of carnal recognition was simply an involuntary response to his hard masculinity, the aura of fiercely primal sexuality that smoked around him and through him. Exciting, even dangerous, but ultimately meaningless unless it was joined with love.

Instead of easing, the storm had intensified. Thunder growled around the horizon and intermittent flashes of lightning lit up the curtained windows as Luke came back into the room.

'Here,' he said, setting his load down on the floor. 'Choose ones that don't crush.'

'They'll survive,' she told him crisply, kneeling beside the heap.

After a moment he said, 'I'll be back shortly.'

Sorrel spread the clothes out into two piles a suitable distance apart. Taking her place on the smaller heap, she discovered a pleased Baggie in residence and turfed him off before curling up on it. The carpeted floor, perfectly comfortable when she'd been sitting on it, metamorphosed into concrete.

It was going to be a long night. She wriggled around

and pulled a knitted jersey over her knees and feet, then rolled several T-shirts into a make-believe pillow.

Closing her eyes, she wooed sleep with eager desperation, every nerve stretched, each cell in her body tense and expectant.

When Luke come back into the room she watched from slitted eyes as he stoked up the fire, and heard him settle onto the pile of clothes she'd arranged. 'Thank you,' he said formally. 'Goodnight, Sorrel.'

'Goodnight,' she said gruffly.

The old house creaked around them. Sorrel listened to the wind and the rain and imagined the flowers being pounded into slush across the garden; she strained to hear the steady, rhythmic sound of Luke's breathing.

Much later Baggie wandered over and curled up against the back of her knees, and eventually she drifted into a restless sleep, waking whenever Luke put wood on the fire and Baggie shifted his allegiance—and his warmth.

Plagued by dreams, she forced her eyes open from one to find herself shivering.

'What's the matter?' Luke asked quietly from the darkness.

She muttered, 'I'm cold.'

He got up to put another load of wood on the fire. Dusting off his hands, he turned to look down at her. 'The wind's gone around to the south, but at least it's driven away the rain.'

Still hazy with sleep, it took her a moment to remember that in the Southern Hemisphere the south was the cold quarter. 'Is the power back on?'

'Not yet.'

His voice was so much closer that her eyes flew open, to see his shape crouching beside her.

'What—?' she asked as he rested the back of his fingers on her cheek. Heat radiated from him and she had to stop herself from following that fleeting touch. She swallowed and finished huskily, 'What's the matter?'

'You're freezing.'

His curt tone flicked her on the raw. He got up and bent to his own pile; Sorrel lifted herself on one elbow and watched incredulously as he scooped up the clothes she'd put there for him and carried them across to her, swearing mildly under his breath when Baggie skipped out of the way.

'What are you doing?' she asked in a high-pitched voice.

'Warming you up.' He dumped the clothes beside hers, lowered himself onto them, and pulled her into the hard, warm cage made by his arms and body.

Heat surged through her—heat from his body and matching heat from hers—driving up through her skin and turning to fever. Sorrel clenched teeth that threatened to chatter.

'Go back to sleep,' he commanded.

Her pulses thudded so loudly in her ears that she had to go over his words in her mind to understand them. When she did she almost laughed. *Go to sleep!* How on earth could she, with him curved around her, making her so fiercely conscious of him she felt as if her nerves were tipped by razors?

Her heart skipped in her breast as she responded to his heat and the sleek, heavily muscled potency of him. Capturing air between lips that had turned warm and sensitive, she forced her breathing into a slow, deliberate pattern, one she'd used hundreds of times before to summon serenity.

This time it didn't work. Instead of calming her senses and her mind, the exercise honed them. She'd never felt so intensely alive.

'Relax,' Luke said, his voice somehow reverberating through her in a frighteningly intimate closeness. 'You're as tense as a violin string.'

She searched for a flippant answer, but her mind remained obstinately in thrall to sensation. In the pit of her stomach those sensations contracted into a knot of need so powerful it was all she could do to stop herself from turning sinuously in his grasp and pressing against him, offering herself.

As though he sensed her thoughts, his arms flexed around her. He said coolly, 'Stop behaving like a virgin, Sorrel. You must know by now that an erection is a perfectly normal response to a situation like this. It doesn't mean that I'm going to tear your clothes off. Just go to sleep.'

Bitter humiliation chilled her, but it didn't eradicate the aching hunger. So she was just another female body—why should that hurt so much?

She lay rigid in his grip until a bone-deep, irresistible tiredness dragged her under. Slowly the turbulent images faded from her mind, until eventually she sank into a deep sleep.

But she dreamed of the night Luke had kissed her. Even in her dream she responded to that kiss—deep, drugging, terrifyingly pleasurable—and this time he didn't pull away, didn't say in a voice savage with self-contempt, 'No!'

And no cool, guarded apology.

This time one kiss turned to two, and then three, and soon she was lost in a dark enchantment. This time, she thought exultantly, there would be no going back...

CHAPTER FOUR

LUKE said her name. 'Sorrel.'

Just one word, yet it was enough to catapult her into instant awareness.

Her eyes flew open, to be captured by the crystalline glitter of his beneath half-closed lids. Above the fire's quiet hiss and crackle she heard her breath catch in her throat, backed by the fierce tattoo of her heart.

And she drowned in the unguarded hunger in Luke's eyes.

No dream, this! They were lying on the heap of clothes in front of the fire at Parenga, and she was strained against him, her taut, expectant body enfolded by his heat and lean, dynamic strength.

Dazed by sleep and drunk with sensation, she yielded to temptation, lifting her mouth to his. He said something, the word muffled by her lips, and then he kissed her again, a fierce claiming that effectively shut down her mind. Need, primitive and stark, gripped her with claws of iron and velvet. She sighed and her fingers tangled in the springy hair at the nape of his neck, pulling him closer, closer.

He raised his head, but even as she made a little protesting noise his lips found her throat. Pulses jumping wildly, she sighed again at the erotic mastery of his kisses. His hand slid up beneath her jersey, finding the taut, slight mound of one breast.

Fire ran through her. She heard her choked whimper as his fingers stroked over the acutely sensitive skin—

heard too the sudden stop in his breathing. A giddy sense of power rocked through her. For once Luke wasn't completely in control. He held her and touched her like a man forced beyond endurance, almost as though he despised himself for wanting her.

Long fingers pushed up the loose material of shirt and jersey. He bent his head and kissed the pleading centre of her breast, so lightly the warmth of his mouth barely registered, yet she shuddered as unbearable excitement sizzled from her breast to the pit of her stomach.

His big frame hardened, the clear evidence of his passion summoning a feverish need. His scent was delicious to her, the coiled tension of his body infinitely stimulating, and she wanted nothing more than to give in to temptation and find exactly what she'd sought all these years. Her hips jerked in an involuntary summons.

Flames spat in the fireplace, sending a flare of light over Luke's profile, the harshly symmetrical angles and lines barely softened by the curve of his mouth against the pale skin of her breast.

Sorrel whispered his name and her hand curved around his face, fingers delighting in the raw silk of his beard and the arrogant contour of cheek and jaw.

He froze, every muscle in his big body locked in denial. She felt his breath shudder across her skin.

'No,' he rasped, and rolled over, levering himself to his feet in a movement that took him across to the fireplace. He stood with his back to her, light flickering around the dark outline of his big body—light that revealed one fist clenched at his side, the other on the mantel.

Humiliation scored her soul. Curling up in a tight

ball like a wounded animal, she realised it had happened again—she'd submitted mindlessly to the silent promise of his hand cupping her breast, his mouth ravishing her thoughts from her mind, and then he'd flung her surrender back in her face.

Just as he'd done ten years previously.

She jack-knifed into a sitting position and hugged her knees, resting her forehead on them as she fought for sanity. This time she was older, more able to deal with rejection. Well, better able to recover from it, anyway.

'You're right. This is—not wise,' she croaked over the silent scream of outrage from her frustrated body.

'But inevitable.' He paused, and when she neither spoke nor lifted her head from her knees he went on in a coldly judicial tone that effectively doused her aching hunger, 'And now I know that your photographs weren't air-brushed into perfection. And that you still kiss like a siren.'

'And you like a conqueror,' she muttered. 'I was asleep, damn you.'

He said coldly, 'Really? I'm not at my most controlled when I wake with a woman in my arms.'

No, not even the extra years made his rejection easier to cope with. She lifted her head and hissed, 'Are you insinuating that I started it?'

He didn't answer immediately. Instead he stooped and picked up a couple of logs, setting them onto the fire with what seemed exaggerated precision while Sorrel seethed.

'No,' he said eventually. 'I don't know who began, and it doesn't matter. What does matter is that it isn't going anywhere. I know too much about your sort of woman.'

'*My sort?*' Her voice cracked. 'So I'm tarred with the same brush as your stepmother? Tell me, do you consider all redheaded women to be greedy and amoral and cruel? Or do we have to have long legs as well, to get the full treatment? And don't you realise that she dyed her hair?'

He said tersely, 'Of course I know. It has nothing to do with looks.'

'So you dislike all women?' Made reckless by anger and pain, she added, 'You can get therapy for that, you know.'

'I am *not* a misogynist.'

Oh, she'd touched a nerve there—he spoke with a gritty fury that warned her to go no further.

'Could have fooled me,' she said crisply, scrambling up. 'I'll be back in a minute.' She headed towards the bathroom, raw with a stabbing hunger.

So now she knew that he'd be a magnificent lover. How many women had he kissed, made love to, to acquire that formidable sexual confidence?

Probably too many to count.

With the bathroom door closed behind her, she stood shivering in the dense darkness and vowed that she wasn't ever going to open herself to that again. Luke couldn't have made it more plain that he desired her only in the most basic way, with the impersonal, animal hunger of a man for a pliant woman—for relief, she thought, sickened.

At least he'd had the decency to call a halt. With stark honesty she admitted that she wouldn't have. She'd been completely lost.

And, decent or not, she hated him for being able to.

But why did he categorise her as the same sort of woman as his stepmother? That really hurt.

The thought of meeting those sardonic eyes tore her composure to tatters, but she stiffened her shoulders. Pride forbade that she spend the rest of the night cowering in the bathroom.

Falling back on techniques she'd learned years before, she began to breathe quietly and deeply, submerging her hurt bewilderment in the regular, comforting process.

When she returned he glanced at her before resuming his grim observation of the flames; as far as she could see he hadn't moved. At least he couldn't see the peaked, ultra-sensitive nipples under the fine wool of her jersey.

Setting her jaw, she began to transfer her small pile of clothes to the other side of the fire.

Luke said, 'I'm going to see if the creek's down enough to get across.' When she looked up he said brusquely, 'Stay there. There's no need for you to come and it's chilly out.'

Sorrel sank down onto her meagre bed and watched him leave the room, Baggie following enthusiastically. Both returned a few minutes later, bringing in a gust of rain and wind and fresh vegetation.

'Not yet,' Luke said briefly. 'See if you can get some more sleep.'

She bit her lip, but she knew what she had to do. 'I'm sorry,' she said quietly.

'Forget about it.' His voice was hard.

But when she was once more lying on her side, courting sleep with dogged determination, he asked pleasantly, 'Who were you kissing, Sorrel?'

She pretended not to hear him. He said nothing more, and after a while she realised that he was asleep.

It seemed the ultimate insult. Here she was, unable

to chisel memories from her mind—the touch of his mouth and experienced fingers, the heat and vibrant power of his body against hers—and he thought so little of what had happened that he could sleep!

You should have known, she reminded herself austerely. You found out ten years ago. One night he kissed you stupid, then he gave you a horrified, stunned look and told you he was sorry, that it meant nothing except that you were a very pretty girl and he was fond of you.

And the next night at a beach barbecue he'd met Mari O'Neill.

Acutely conscious of him—and still hopeful that he'd been chivalrous because she was so much younger—Sorrel had seen the glint in Luke's eyes when he'd repeated the newcomer's name in a deep, sexy voice with a note in it she'd never heard before.

Mari, a small blonde with curves and huge dark eyes, had glanced at him through her lashes in a way she'd probably intended to be demure. Luke had smiled down at her, the intent appreciation in his grey eyes barely concealing a purely male speculation.

And Sorrel had accepted with sick finality that the kiss that had fuelled her fantasies the previous night truly had meant nothing to him; her hopes and dreams were doomed to die.

Trying desperately not to let anyone see her misery, she had smiled her way through that evening, inwardly writhing with awareness of the two of them in their own cocoon of mutual attraction.

A couple of days later Mari had come up to her in the main street of the nearest small town, and asked bluntly, 'Is there anything between you and Luke Hardcastle?'

'No,' Sorrel told her, head high.

Mari gave a short, satisfied nod. 'I didn't think there could be, but he was so protective the other night at the barbecue I wondered if there was more to your relationship than the big brother thing.' She shrugged and explained, 'I don't poach, so I wanted to make sure.'

From some hidden reservoir Sorrel dredged up a gritty courage that allowed her to say, 'You're not poaching.' She added with a spark of malice, 'But even if you want to it will be Luke who makes the decision.'

Mari laughed, a sensuous sound that held a wealth of knowledge. 'You haven't got a mother, have you?'

'No.'

'Then think of me as an older sister for a moment and remember this. It's always the woman who chooses.'

Not in Luke's case, Sorrel thought.

Within a week they were a couple. Wounded to the soul, Sorrel gave in to her father's suggestion that she enter a modelling competition, and when, astonishingly, she won it she accepted the contract with an agency in New York and left Luke and Parenga far behind.

Sorrel woke to the sun poking thin shafts of light through the drawn curtains, and the rushing noise of the river streaming by into the estuary. A glance at her watch revealed that it was a couple of hours after sunrise.

Yawning, she stretched, the slow burn of aching muscles reminding her that she'd spent the night on the floor. She was alone, lying in a heap of tumbled clothes. The fire had died down to ashes and Baggie, traitor that he was, had left with Luke.

Oh, God—Luke! She scrambled up and pulled back the curtains, standing in a golden box of sunlight to assess the carnage in the garden. The magnolia had been stripped of its glory of pink and white, but dark blue irises unfurled beneath, and she noted the buds of daylilies, storm-proof and gallant, glowing in the sunlight.

And next year the magnolia would flower again.

So learn that lesson, she commanded herself, turning away. She was every bit as tough as it was.

In the kitchen she found her suitcases on the floor, and a note on the bench.

The creek's down but the power's not on yet because the road's still closed. Come along to the homestead to shower and for breakfast. Baggie's with me.

After a fuming few moments Sorrel decided to accept what was more of a command than an invitation, but only because she desperately needed a shower.

After she'd changed into a cowl-necked jersey of fine caramel wool, and tailored trousers in a darker shade, she pulled leather boots onto her feet and made a mental memo to buy herself a pair of proper gumboots. Garnering up her toiletries and a pair of briefs, she dropped them into a carry-bag and went out into the fresh morning.

Before she left, however, she tried a light switch, pulling a face at its futile click, amending Luke's mocking words to *No power, no water, no shower.*

Although the creek was no longer the voracious monster of the night before it still hurried along, laden with rich red-brown soil. Sorrel picked her way through the layer of silt over the bridge, stretching her legs so that she walked in Luke's footprints.

Striding down the road and breathing in great lungfuls of air heavy with the scent of rain-soaked vegetation and the river and sea, she told herself she had no need to be embarrassed about seeing him again.

OK, so coming back to Parenga was proving to be more—*challenging*—than she'd expected, but she could cope with Luke's obvious distaste for her. Although she'd like to know the reason for it. Surely he didn't really think she was like his stepmother?

She'd disliked Cherie, but then, no one had liked her, and Luke certainly had good reason to despise her.

But to judge Sorrel purely on the basis of their shared hair colour—no, it was ridiculous. He was far too logical to do that.

Who understood what Luke thought beneath that iron reserve? Certainly not her. But, in case he thought she was intent on an affair, she'd make it obvious she hadn't come back to Parenga with any designs on his magnificent body! A quick smile tugged at her lips. Last night had been a mistake, but they had both been asleep…

After all these years she still wanted him. Her smile hardened into irony. She might be safe from him, but how safe was she from herself?

'Perfectly safe,' she said abruptly. 'All you have to remember is the look on his face when he realised who he was making love to. That was a passion-killer if ever I've seen one!'

But deep inside she ached for something she'd never had, never would have.

Movement along the road caught her eye. Baggie,

fur fluffed out, tail held high, paced towards her with sedate complacency.

'Well, hello,' she greeted him, bending to scratch behind his splendid tufted ears. 'You're looking a lot more cheerful this morning!'

He suffered her caress for a few seconds before wriggling away to eye a cheeky fantail in the bottom branches of a huge, ancient camellia tree. 'Don't even think about it,' Sorrel warned. 'Birds are not on your menu.'

But, apart from his obsession with eels, Baggie wasn't a serious hunter. He accompanied her graciously, even stopping further on when she peered between massive old flame trees to the river, smooth and brown and muscular, splitting around the island on its way to spill into the sea.

Her spirits lifting, Sorrel smiled as a tui wooed a mate amongst the spidery orange flowers of a grevillea. Gleaming iridescent blue-green, with a lacy white cape around its shoulders and a bobble of white at its throat, the bird posed and strutted and capered in front of its lady, producing an eccentric collection of whirrs and clicks interspersed with glorious liquid trills like a miniature carillon.

'Stick to the bells,' Sorrel advised him wryly. 'Sweet beats sour every time. Right, Baggie?'

Baggie ignored her to turn his head and gaze behind them.

A second later Sorrel's less acute hearing picked up the subdued clop of hooves. Her heart jumped when Luke rode around the corner, both he and his big bay gelding tiger-striped by the bars of sunlight sifting through the leaves.

He was wearing a thin black crew-necked jersey and

dark trousers, wet to the knees. Relaxed, yet alert, he looked like a warrior from a time out of myth, when battle-hardened barbarians fought for a code of honour as rigid and enduring as their armour.

'Good morning,' Sorrel said, her mouth suddenly dry as she looked up into his bronzed, unyielding face.

The gelding bent its head to nuzzle Baggie, then straightened up to switch a cursory tail over its flanks. Sorrel stepped back; at any other time she'd have enjoyed the familiar earthy smell of horse and leather, but not just now.

'Good morning.' Luke surveyed her in leisurely assessment. 'When I left you looked as though you were ready to sleep for another eight hours.'

Colour heated her skin, but she managed a composed smile. 'What time did you wake?'

He swung down and led the horse towards her, stooping a moment to stroke an importunate Baggie. Straightening up, he said, 'Daybreak. You've got shadows under your eyes. Sleeping on the floor obviously doesn't agree with you. I'll ring the council and tell them to get the road cleared as soon as they can. Once they've done that the power authority can fix the line, and then you'll be able to organise some furniture.'

'Just like that?' she asked sweetly. 'You snap your fingers and the council jumps?'

His broad shoulders lifted and the smile that curled his chiselled mouth was both compelling and ironic. 'If there aren't more important slips to clear. It certainly won't hurt to let them know we're without both communications and power.'

As well as expecting his orders to be obeyed, Luke was a man who took charge. Not, however, of her life. Pronouncing each word with clarity and determination, she said, 'I'll borrow your mobile phone, if that's all right, and ring them myself.'

'Why?' Luke asked casually.

'Because it's my problem,' she told him with more curtness than she'd intended. 'I'll bet you've got a generator for emergencies like this.'

'Of course. The equipment sheds and barns are on this line too, so a generator's a necessity.'

Sorrel tightened her mouth, her gaze direct and unwavering. 'I'll deal with it. I'm grown up now,' she said steadily. 'I don't need a big brother or a mentor.'

Something burned fiercely blue in his eyes. 'I don't feel like either,' he said austerely. 'Perhaps you've been away from New Zealand for so long you've forgotten that neighbours help each other whenever they can.'

She sent him a limpid look. 'You're sounding a bit insular, Luke. Good neighbours exist all around the world.'

When the gelding lowered its head and whickered softly, Luke lifted a lean tanned hand to stroke its nose. 'We'd better get going; he wants his breakfast and you, I imagine, want a shower.' Lightly, easily, he swung up onto the horse, muscles flexing smoothly beneath his cotton shirt. From this position of power he surveyed her. 'Want to get up behind me?'

She shook her head. 'Baggie and I will walk, thank you,' she said coolly.

That was how she'd lost her heart to Luke—when he'd offered her a ride down the hot, dusty road a few days after she'd come back from the modelling course. Until then it had just been the classic schoolgirl crush, almost sexless. But that hot, languorous day she'd been beguiled into first love by the sheer physical pleasure of sitting behind him with her arms around his waist, dreamily listening to his steady heartbeat, her nostrils filled with the fascinating scent of man and horse, dusty road and wild ginger flowers.

Luke remembered too, she could tell. He broke eye contact only when the horse moved restlessly beneath him. Sorrel watched his strong legs clamp its girth as he controlled the big animal.

'I'll see you at the homestead,' she said in a voice that had gone suddenly rough.

He sketched a salute that approached a taunt, clicked his tongue at the gelding, and left her.

Reluctantly Sorrel followed, wondering whether riding like a centaur came naturally or was the result of being tossed onto a horse before you could walk, as Luke had once told her he'd been.

The last time she'd walked along this road he'd been living in an old caravan in a paddock above the river. He could have turned a family out of one of the four farm cottages, but Luke's rigorous conscience wouldn't allow that. The formidable fire that burned beneath his controlled façade, its source the same determination that had driven him to bring Waimanu back to its former glory, meant that he'd been the one to suffer the substandard conditions.

It hadn't taken him long to turn Waimanu around. Over the years Cynthia had faithfully relayed to her his hard work, his successes, and his growing reputation as a businessman with solid ties to the land and innovative ideas about its use.

For Luke, fired by dynamic energy and an inborn love for the land, Waimanu would be the only place to build. The new homestead would be his validation, the final crown, replacing the house he'd been forced to sell and wiping out the last remnants of his step-mother's legacy of mismanagement.

Deep in thought, Sorrel walked out of the tunnel of trees onto a wide sealed area—and stopped.

As a model she'd been photographed in glorious houses all over the world; as a minor celebrity she'd gone to parties and stayed weekends at splendid mansions. But something about this one, settled into gardens that looked as though they'd been there for ever, caught at her heart.

Not that it was a mansion. Modern, designed by an immense talent, the large double-storeyed house fitted like a jewel into the primal setting of garden, river and the fertile hills of Waimanu station. Sorrel swivelled to note a vast garage, connected at right angles to the house, with what seemed to be living quarters above. An island of lush plantings divided the sealed concourse, a more disciplined garden separating the drive and the house.

She let out a long, soft sigh of delighted appreciation—replaced by a surge of adrenalin as Luke strolled around the corner of the garage.

Baggie made a cheerful sound halfway between a purr and meow and set off towards him, tail waving in greeting.

Deliberately relaxing tight muscles, Sorrel composed her face to hide the mixture of apprehension and heady pleasure that warred inside her. Luke took up too much space—in every way.

Yet her eyes lingered on the way the sun bathed him in a shimmering aura. Its warm light should have subdued the uncompromising impact of his silent, graceful stride and the ruthless lines of his face. It didn't. Starkly compelling, he projected a tough maleness that sent a shiver scudding down her spine.

Gesturing at the house, she said, 'Luke, this is *perfect* for Waimanu.'

'Thank you,' he said evenly, a territorial inflection giving the words an edge that made her glance sharply at him. 'The architect did an excellent job. I decided to build it when Cynthia told me she wasn't going to sell Parenga back to me.'

Iron-grey eyes, burnished and unreadable, clashed with hers.

Sorrel turned her head and pretended to examine the façade, following its gracious, welcoming lines. 'That must have annoyed you.'

'A little, but I'm not sentimental,' he said smoothly, watching her with a hard intensity that pulled every tiny hair on her skin upright.

Sorrel looked away. 'I know plants grow fast in Northland, but these seem well established. Surely they're older than the house?'

Luke began to walk towards the garage. 'I had the gardens planted a year or so after you left.'

Something about the way he spoke set alarm bells ringing, but as she set off after him Sorrel couldn't for the life of her work out why. Landscaping a couple of hectares wasn't exactly a deeply significant action.

Another tui set up a musical clamour in the gold-dipped branch of a kowhai. Luke slowed until Sorrel caught him up, then said, 'I took the perishables from your car and put them in the fridge inside. They were still cold, so they should be all right.'

'I seem to be saying thank you all the time.' The scent of flowers and greenery, of Luke—salt and male mixed with the faintest touch of horse—set her senses buzzing as she went with him towards the garage.

He'd parked her middle-aged vehicle inside, thoroughly out of place between a sleekly opulent BMW and the Land Rover.

'Come in,' he invited, and opened the connecting door into the house.

CHAPTER FIVE

'THIS way,' Luke indicated, mouth quirking at the predatory gleam in Baggie's eyes as the cat paced with dignity towards a container of dry food. 'We'll leave him to enjoy his breakfast—it's the only way we'll get to have ours in peace.'

'Thank you very much for taking care of him,' Sorrel said.

'He's no problem—he's a very self-contained cat except for his over-developed tendency to dramatise,' Luke said drily, and opened another door into the interior of the house.

Sorrel walked past both cat and man into a passage that led towards the front of the house. Even that utilitarian area breathed a subtle, unstudied comfort, but the front hall it led into was magnificent, with a superb flight of stairs soaring up to the next floor.

Luke took her up and opened a door a few metres along a light-filled hall. 'The spare bedroom,' he said laconically, adding with a swift, flashing grin that cut her foolish heart adrift, 'It has an *en suite* bathroom.'

'I am so looking forward to that,' Sorrel said with real gratitude, admiring the decoration in warm vanilla and cream with smoky shades of chocolate and claret for accents. 'I feel grubby and dehydrated and a shower is long overdue.'

'Whereas you look cool and very much in control,' he said evenly. 'The towels are in the bathroom— through that door there. Breakfast in half an hour.'

'Thank you. This is very kind of you—especially as my stupidity cost you an uncomfortable night.'

'Country hospitality,' he said briefly. 'No thanks necessary.'

He didn't actually say, Nothing personal, but he was making sure she understood that. Not that he had to—Sorrel recognised a rejection when it was flung in her face.

Once the door closed behind him she let out a long breath and decamped into the bathroom.

Fifteen minutes later she emerged, rosy from a luxurious wallow, dark hair silky and dry. Sensuously relishing her clean skin and underwear, she pulled on the cowl top and trousers.

For some reason she felt more alert than she had for years, more vital and vigorous. Perhaps it was being back in New Zealand, she thought, wryly aware that, much as she loved her homeland, it wasn't the reason for this singing in her blood.

It took ten minutes to craft a face that looked—well, she'd tried for serenity, but the mirror revealed a soft lick of colour along her high cheekbones and a turbulence in her eyes that no cosmetics could disguise.

'Who cares? He certainly doesn't,' she said aloud, closing her case.

Luke was striding along the hall when she came out of the bedroom. He'd showered and changed too; lean, powerful body supple in a T-shirt and another well-cut pair of trousers, he looked at her with a disturbing glitter of awareness. 'Hungry?'

'Yes.' She wondered why he'd leashed that simmering antagonism. Whatever Luke did, he did for a reason. 'I hope your housekeeper doesn't mind my food in the fridge.'

'Why should she?'

Oops. Lightly she explained, 'Most women get possessive about their workplace. I know people who don't dare go into their own kitchen because their treasured cook might take umbrage.'

'The fridge belongs to me,' he said crisply, 'and so does the food in it—except yours, of course. Penn isn't so foolish as to object. What would you like to eat?'

'Scrambled eggs,' Sorrel told him, 'and I'll cook them. I do really good scrambled eggs.'

Fifteen minutes later Luke said with lazy appreciation, '"Really good" doesn't convey the perfection of those eggs. Where did you learn to cook like that?'

'Cynthia's special technique.' Sorrel smiled, absurdly pleased by the compliment. 'When I was about twelve she was horrified to find out I couldn't do anything more than make toast and heat tinned food. She took me in hand.'

'Do you remember your mother?'

Startled, she looked across the table. Sunlight, scooped into the pleasant living and dining room by wide east-facing windows, burnished his olive skin, emphasising the bold framework that gave his face its strength and power.

He was watching her from beneath lashes that most women would kill for. Yet, long and black and thickly curling though they were, they didn't soften his face any more than the classical perfection of his mouth did. Luke looked exactly what he was—part buccaneer, part tycoon, and all hard, uncompromising male.

'Just snatches,' she said, pouring herself a cup of coffee. The homely little task gave her something to do with hands that itched to trace the outline of his mouth. 'I was four when she died, but I can remember her singing to me, and laughing with my father. And how empty our house was afterwards. Dad did his best, but nothing was ever the same again. He told me once he'd never met another woman he could love like he loved my mother.'

'Cynthia said he wasn't able to settle after that,' Luke said in a non-committal tone.

'He was always restless, always moving on,' she said defensively, wondering now if it had been gambling debts that had driven him away from each place. 'I think he got worse after my mother died.'

'So you lived a nomadic life.'

'Well—yes. But he did his best for me. I was cared for, and I knew he loved me. Do you remember your mother?'

'Very well.' Luke got to his feet and walked across the room to open the French windows onto a terrace overlooking the garden. Looking out over his domain, he said levelly, 'I was eight when she escaped from Waimanu.'

Sorrel bit her lip. 'I didn't know,' she murmured.

He gave her a swift, unreadable glance over his shoulder. 'That she left my father?' he drawled. 'I'm surprised local gossip didn't fill you in on the juicy details. She married a rich Australian who didn't expect her to live at the back of beyond. She's still with him, as far as I know.'

'As far as you know?' she asked, wondering what he meant.

'I've only seen her a few times since she left Waimanu.'

Shocked, Sorrel stared at him. 'Did your father refuse to let you go overseas?'

Luke shrugged. 'She didn't want to see me,' he said coolly.

What sort of woman would leave her child behind? 'I didn't know,' she said again, tentatively.

'It didn't make much difference; I was a proper little savage, out on the station with Dad whenever I could be.'

And what sort of answer was that?

The only one she was going to get.

Luke suddenly stooped to pick up a tennis ball, hurling it with speed and deadly accuracy at a hawk swooping low across the lawn towards helpless prey—a duck anxiously shepherding her brood up from the riverbank.

The ball landed exactly where he'd aimed it, close by the duck, and bounced high, scaring off the hawk. It soared into the air again and flew above the river towards the other side.

'Well done,' Sorrel applauded from the table, hoping he wouldn't note the false note in her voice. The swift, explosive power of his reaction had released a flood of hot response in her, something so raw and unexpected she shook with it.

She'd become a connoisseur of men's bodies after working with male models who spent hours each day in the gym, buffing and shaping their muscles set by set until they reached a peak of physical perfection. Luke had probably never set foot in a gym. Broad-shouldered, narrow-hipped and long of leg, his body had been shaped by years of punishingly hard work in the sun and rain.

And she wanted him so badly she could feel the need splintering through her—this man, only this man.

Only *ever* Luke.

Over the years she'd met nice men, sexy men,

charming men, rich men, even a few dangerously attractive men; not one had roused anything more than her mild interest. She'd even thought she'd loved a couple of them, yet making love had always been a disappointment.

But Luke—a man she didn't even like much—could make her stomach turn over with a glance and melt her bones every time he touched her.

Wide-eyed and stunned, she stared at him as he turned back towards the room. The sun gilded his tanned skin and black hair, warming those grey eyes with their rare, fugitive flash of blue. Beneath his sculpted face and the physical perfection of that big body there glowed a dark fire, an inborn sexual expertise instantly recognised by any woman who set eyes on him.

Her breath came fast through trembling lips. Sorrel lifted her coffee cup and drank. Was she so shallow that sex meant more to her than all the other things she valued in a man—love, respect, kindness, intelligence…?

No. But what made Luke different from any other man?

'I have to admire the hawk—it's nothing if not persistent,' he said, strolling inside to sit down again. 'And the ducklings make it so easy—they're imprinted to follow their mother in a single file. The hawk would take every duckling if someone didn't intervene; as it is, between it and the eels not many survive, but I do try to redress the balance.'

She tried hard for light irony, relieved when her voice came out a little stiff but without a quaver. 'It's charming to see you display your nurturing side.'

He shot her a keen look and her brain made a connection, homing in on that elusive difference.

Luke's face and bearing, the tone of his deep voice and his choice of words, every action—even the way he wore his clothes with such casual confidence—signalled a man who could be trusted to deliver on any promise he made. He didn't have to proclaim his competence—it was simply there, like his formidable intelligence and rock-solid integrity.

Perhaps she was like those ducklings, Sorrel thought with a desperation that came close to panic. Perhaps she'd been imprinted at such an early age that no man would ever measure up to Luke.

A bleak grief shivered through her. No, that was ridiculous; she was exaggerating her normal reaction to a very sexy man she'd met at an impressionable stage of her life. Every woman remembered her first love.

All she had to do was remember that, although she might be obsessed by the past, he'd moved on.

And so would she.

'Something wrong with the coffee?' Luke asked blandly.

Sorrel blinked. 'Sorry?'

His smile didn't reach the metallic grey eyes. 'You've been holding the cup in mid-air since I came back in.'

'It's delicious.' Hastily she took a sip, before putting the cup down to improvise, 'I hope it won't take too long for them to clear the slip on the road.'

'Don't worry about it.'

'Easy enough for you to say, with your thumping great generator!' she retorted crisply. 'Lovely though this house is, I want to go home to Parenga.'

He held her gaze for two of the longest seconds of

her life, before he glanced at his watch. 'I'll give
Forbes a ring now.'

Sorrel said evenly, 'I'll do—'

He got to his feet, deliberately towering over her.
'Sorrel, just drink the rest of that coffee, all right? I
have to contact my farm manager—make sure that
everyone in the cottages is all right, that sort of thing.
It's going to take me all of two minutes to ring the
council after that.'

She said between her teeth, 'Stop interrupting me.
It's rude, it's a form of bullying, and I won't put up
with it.'

Much to her indignation he nodded. 'OK, it's a bad
habit. Blame it on being an only child.'

When Sorrel snorted, he laughed softly and flicked
a careless finger along her cheekbone as he went by
her chair.

Which was just as well, because he didn't see the
havoc that light, insulting touch made of her composure. Heat flooded up through her skin and her hand
shook so much she almost spilt the coffee.

She gulped down the rest and got to her feet to pace
across the room with swift, silent steps. Surely the
power line would be repaired soon? Duelling with Luke
was perilously exhilarating, but every minute she
stayed in his house was another hole punched in her
defences.

Restlessly she walked out onto the terrace, staring
over the bright lawn to the red-brown gleam of the river
through a screen of shrubs and trees. Bees hummed
amongst flowers, the hawk flew high in the blue sky,
and the cold patch in her stomach expanded.

Perhaps she should turn her back on Luke and
Parenga—just walk away and leave before she got in

too deep. From the wreckage of her affairs she'd saved enough money to survive for a very frugal six months; fewer if she had to find another place to live. She could manage that. And although she probably wouldn't be able to resurrect her career, she might find a job in fashion somewhere.

Except that she didn't want to go back to that world, and if she left Parenga she'd be letting Cynthia down; for some reason it had been important to her godmother that she spend six months here.

Her head came up unconsciously and her lips firmed. For Cynthia she would do it, Luke or no.

When he was near she might flutter like a moth snared by the fatal fascination of a candle, but she was safe enough; he didn't want her.

She went back inside and began to clear the table. When he returned she'd just lifted the marmalade pot in one hand, the jug of orange juice in the other.

'Hardcastle Road is well down the list,' he said aloofly. 'They didn't know you were back, of course, but even so other roads have more people living on them. And until McLeod's Hill is cleared the power board can't get in.'

Frowning, she elbowed open the door between the family room and kitchen. 'How long will that take?'

'Probably not until tomorrow morning.'

She spluttered, 'That's outrageous!'

'You're in the north of New Zealand,' he said, a whiplash of contempt slicing into her. 'The world doesn't revolve around you. Yesterday's storm was a bad one, and coming after a long, dry spell it's created mayhem. It doesn't matter anyway—you can stay here until the power's restored.'

Cynically Luke waited for her to protest; she didn't

disappoint him. Her eyes narrowed, the black lashes concentrating their pale clarity into green-gold crystals. Her chin lifted, and the luscious mouth that had fuelled millions of feverish male fantasies tightened.

Her voice, however, was patient. 'Thank you for the invitation, but that won't be necessary. I can manage.'

'How?' he demanded, clamping down on a hot spurt of anger. 'In a house with no furniture, no blankets, nothing to keep you warm except a fireplace?' He paused before adding deliberately, 'And that's not counting the lack of water and sewage.'

Luke's eyes narrowed as she sauntered into the kitchen, hips swaying in the seductive movement that still figured in his dreams. Silently he cursed the involuntary tightening of every muscle in his body. He began to collect the utensils.

From the other side of the door she said quietly, 'It's not your problem, Luke.'

He strode through into the kitchen. 'If it were Cynthia, would you expect me to leave her there?' He waited for the next objection, wondering why he bothered. Why not just let her go back to Parenga, muddle uncomfortably around until the road opened and she could get Cynthia's furniture out of storage? She was nothing to him.

Nothing but trouble.

He despised himself for wanting her, even in this uncomplicated, purely sexual way. He shouldn't have held her sleek, fragrant body in his arms last night, calling up old memories, an old hunger...

Yet he couldn't just let her go.

'That's different,' she parried. 'Cynthia was old. No one would expect her to sleep on the floor!' She changed tack. 'It's very kind of you, but—'

'I'm not kind,' he told her, the words echoing in her mind.

Steadying her voice, she said, 'Listen to me, Luke! I can't just dump myself on you.'

'Unless you camp in the car or go back and sleep on the floor at Parenga, you can't do anything else,' he said curtly, dumping the utensils onto the granite counter. 'And either of those would be cutting off your nose to spite your face.'

He was right, damn him. Grabbing at her self-possession, she said formally, 'If I could just borrow a mattress—'

'I have no spares.'

Furious, she expostulated, 'This house must have at least four bedrooms.'

'Five.' His eyes mocked her.

Sorrel said jerkily, 'Then surely I can borrow a mattress?'

'No,' he said, his voice coldly final. 'Apart from mine, the only other room that's furnished is the one you showered in. Stop it, Sorrel. You're going to have to come along here for meals and to wash, so you might as well sleep here too.'

Sorrel seethed. One glance at his face told her he wasn't going to yield. Luke was a hard man, but he had an inbuilt protectiveness she had no answer to.

'As dictatorial as ever,' she said stiffly. 'I'm not a mother duck, Luke, nor one of those helpless fluffy ducklings.'

He divined the cause of her reluctance and disposed of it with rapid ruthlessness. 'But you see me as a predator, like the hawk. Surely last night showed you that you're quite safe with me?' His mouth curled in contempt. 'I won't demand any payment if you accept the offer of a bed here.'

His cold gaze and flinty features told her exactly how little impact she had on him. Well, she was immune to him—except for that brutally physical response, and she wasn't going to surrender to it. She wanted much more from a man than emotionless sex, however magnificent it might be.

Controlling the chaotic mix of emotions that rampaged through her, she said coolly, 'I certainly don't expect you to demand that I sleep with you in return for the loan of a bed.'

Beyond a compression of his wide, arrogantly outlined mouth he didn't show any surprise at her frankness. 'Then you have no reason to go back to Parenga until you've got furniture and utilities.'

Her eyes clashed with his uncompromising gaze. Sorrel raised hers heavenwards, but accepted as gracefully as she could. 'Thank you.' Then spoilt it all by adding, 'You're as stubborn as a pig.'

'So I've been told,' he said blandly. 'That's settled, then.'

Trying—and failing—to tap into the core of serenity she'd worked so long to acquire, Sorrel opened the door under the sink and peered into the interior of the cupboard.

'Leave those,' he commanded when he saw her pull out the detergent.

'Why?' She straightened up and sent him a belligerent stare.

'Most of them go into the dishwasher, and those that don't the housekeeper will do.'

Sorrel squirted liquid into the sink. 'You stack the

dishwasher and I'll do these,' she said crisply. 'How will your housekeeper get here? By balloon?'

'She lives over the garage, so she'll just walk down some stairs and in the back door.' He glanced at his watch. 'In fact she'll be here shortly.'

It was too intimate, doing this. Sorrel remembered other occasions, nights when Cynthia had asked him along for dinner and fussed a little over him—fussing he'd endured with a smile because, as Cynthia had once observed to Sorrel, 'He knows it makes me feel better about buying the homestead from him!'

He'd been so young to assume the burden of responsibility for Waimanu, but he'd never asked for sympathy. And he'd been astute and unsentimental enough to make hard decisions like selling Parenga so he could use the money to drag his inheritance out of its mire of mismanagement.

The sound of the door opening made Sorrel turn; a woman in her mid-forties came into the room. The smile on her face froze when she saw Sorrel, but only for a second—she replaced it with an enquiring glance at Luke, who was carrying butter and honey across to the refrigerator.

He said, 'Sorrel, this is Penn Turner, who keeps the place running. She is Parenga's owner, Penn, but Sorrel will be staying here until the power comes back on.'

Sorrel and Penn exchanged greetings, and then the housekeeper, a pretty, dark-haired woman with wide blue eyes and a ready smile, bustled into the kitchen and said, 'I'll do that!'

'It's all right,' Sorrel said automatically.

Smiling with polite determination, Penn made shooing motions. 'Guests at Waimanu do not do the dishes!'

She looked at the pile on the bench and said, 'Or stack the dishwasher! Off you go!'

Sorrel stepped back, surrendering with an inward smile at the smaller woman. 'Of course,' she said lightly, and walked out of the kitchen through the door that Luke held open.

He followed her silently, but when they turned a corner in the hall he asked, 'What's the problem?'

He'd always been able to read her mind. 'It's not *my* problem.' She lowered her voice, mimicking his. '"Sorrel will be staying." A classic male statement—on a par with, *Darling, I've just brought ten friends home for dinner!* No query about whether the food will stretch far enough.'

'I pay Penn to deal with that.' His smile was edged. 'And I'm sure no famous model worries about cooking dinner when her lover of the moment wanders in with a guest. Surely that's what restaurants are for?'

'You have a restaurant close by?' she asked sarcastically.

'We always have plenty of food in store.' His shrug indicated that this was completely unimportant to him. 'What would you like to do today?'

'I'm going to start cleaning Parenga.'

His brows met together across the blade of his nose. 'What?'

'You heard. The house needs cleaning.'

'It also needs painting and a fair few minor repairs—repairs that should have been done over the past two years—and the garden needs a considerable amount of attention,' he pointed out relentlessly. 'Are you planning to do all that too?'

Clearly he thought she had the strength and stamina—not to mention the brains—of a jellyfish. Sorrel said crisply, 'Some of it. I certainly don't plan to sit around and paint my toenails. Now, if you show me where the sheets are kept I'll make my bed in the spare bedroom.'

'Do you remember how?' he drawled.

She looked him directly in the eye. 'Why are you being offensive?' she said without a tremor. 'Of course I remember—I make my own bed every morning! Do you?'

'Yes.' He glanced at his watch. 'I've got a phone call due, but if you'll give me five minutes I'll see that the sheets get to you.'

She started up the stairs, suddenly so angry that she couldn't stay with him. Halfway up she stopped and turned, leaning over the banister. He was watching her, his face dark and closed. In a syrupy voice she said, 'It's time you realised I'm all grown up and that I know what I'm doing.'

'You've always known that,' he said indifferently, adding with a glance that pierced her composure like a sword-blade, 'Most women seem to be born knowing it.'

'Now that,' she said, straightening up, 'sounds very close to misogyny.'

'I don't hate women.'

'But you don't trust them.'

With the kind of smile a lion probably bestowed before opening its jaws on its prey, he said, 'I trust anyone who's earned it.'

An icy chill ran down her spine as he swung on his heel and disappeared into a room along the hall.

Five minutes later she'd stripped the covers from the bed, and was setting out the contents of her sponge bag

in the bathroom when she heard a knock on the outside door.

It was Luke, armed with a pile of linen. He ignored
her outstretched hands and dumped the sheets and pil-
lowcases on the elegant bench at the foot of the bed.

Footsteps along the hall, accompanied by the calling
of his name, summoned him. 'Telephone!' Penn announced. 'It's Mr Sutherland—you said he was important.'

He stood for a moment, face expressionless, before
turning. 'I'll be right down.'

As the door closed behind him Sorrel hastily sorted
through the sheets and made the bed. She was smoothing out the claret coverlet when there was another
knock at the door.

'Come in,' she called, expecting Penn.

It wasn't the housekeeper; Luke stood in the doorway, brows drawn together.

'What's the matter?' she asked quickly.

The frown deepened. 'Nothing,' he said. 'I'm going
to Auckland.'

'How?'

'Chopper,' he said succinctly. 'Do you want to
come?'

'No, thank you,' she said in her most precise voice.
'I'll be fine.'

'I won't be back tonight, but Penn will look after
you.'

'I don't need looking after,' Sorrel said, a hint of
frost in her tone, adding with a wry smile, 'But I have
to admit I'd rather sleep in this lovely bed than on the
floor at Parenga.'

He gave a tight smile. 'So would I,' he said, in a
voice that made her look up sharply.

For a moment memories of the night before flooded Sorrel's brain; colour ran like fire through her skin, but she lifted her chin aggressively. Luke's gaze moved to her mouth and then back up to clash with hers.

'Have a good trip,' she said harshly.

Without a word he went out, closing the door behind him.

Heart racing, Sorrel sat down on the edge of the bed, her long fingers caressing the richly coloured silk. Last night in Luke's arms had been heaven, and it meant far too much; if she let her busy mind dwell on it she could recall everything.

And that she couldn't afford to do.

Another knock on the door brought her across the room. This room, she decided as she flung open the door, was getting more like O'Hare Airport every minute!

But it was Penn. 'Oh,' she said in a startled voice, 'you've made the bed! I was just coming in to do it.'

'I don't want to give you any extra work.' Sorrel wished she could rid herself of this feeling that the other woman had taken an instant dislike to her.

'Well, that's my job.' Penn smiled tolerantly. 'I'll come back and do the bathroom when you're out.'

'I can do that too,' Sorrel told her.

The older woman's smile set. 'I don't think Luke would appreciate his guests doing the housework,' she said with a light little laugh. 'It's all right—I don't pry.'

'I didn't—I'm sure you don't.' Round two, Sorrel thought dourly, to the housekeeper. Closing the door, she shrugged. Eventually Penn would realise that she wasn't fighting. In the meantime she was going back to Parenga. She needed time out.

Setting her jaw, she set off down the stairs. She'd

almost reached the bottom when she heard a slight sound and saw a door open along the hall. Luke strode through, stopping when he saw her. He stood in shadow, but she sensed his intent, focused attention, and in spite of everything she was fiercely glad she'd learned to walk with such casual grace.

And that was another dangerous reaction...

'I'm off,' she said, directing a restrained smile in his direction without quite meeting his eyes.

Abruptly Luke said, 'Penn seems to think you've accused her of prying.'

'I'm sorry if she thought that.' Sorrel frowned, trying to recall exactly what she'd said. 'I told her that I'd do the bathroom because I don't want to make any extra work for her, not because I don't trust her.'

'That's her job,' Luke pointed out, adding deliberately, 'You surprise me.'

'Because I'm capable of cleaning a bathroom?' she returned, her voice rising slightly. 'I've stayed in the occasional house that has servants, and in hotels, of course, but in New York I had my own apartment, and although there was a house-cleaning service I did quite a lot of it myself when I was there.' She lifted a brow and finished acidly, not caring that she'd let her irritation get the better of her, 'Have a great time in Auckland.'

Steadily, body poised and relaxed, she took the final step, irritated because it destroyed her temporary advantage of superior height, and walked past him with her back so erect she thought she heard her spine complain.

She felt his eyes boring into the sensitive part between her shoulderblades until she disappeared around the corner.

Why did Penn want to make trouble?

CHAPTER SIX

IN THE midst of scrutinising the main bedroom at Parenga, Sorrel heard the *whump, whump, whump* of helicopter rotors turning. She blinked as the engine noise increased to a shriek, and ran across to the windows, pushing them open to the sunny air to crane out.

She couldn't see the chopper take off, but she heard it rising high to clear the hills. What had called Luke to Auckland?

'None of your business,' she said aloud, and stooped to stroke Baggie.

Almost immediately she straightened up and looked around the room again. She had work to do.

'I'd better make a list,' she said to the cat, who'd taken up residence in a patch of sunlight.

He bestowed her a narrow, long-suffering look, and after an elaborate stretch and a wide yawn that displayed his splendid teeth subsided back into sleep. Smiling, Sorrel ran down the stairs to unearth her handheld computer, a relic from the days when she'd needed all the help she could to keep up with appointments.

Two hours later a cold, unpleasant ball of worry consolidated beneath her ribs as she scrolled down the screen. She hadn't bargained on having to make so many repairs to Parenga. And those were only the visible ones; there were bound to be more she hadn't noticed.

How much would it cost?

'Cleaning first,' she told Baggie, then frowned. 'I

wish the road was open—I need stuff. Oh, well, I'll see if I can borrow a bucket and some detergent from Luke's rather obstructive housekeeper so I can start after lunch.' She glanced at her watch. 'Which I'd better get back to!'

The meal was scheduled for midday, so she just had time to walk along to Waimanu.

At Luke's house she paused inside the back door and listened. Silence and stillness enveloped her, isolating her from warmth and life, telling her in some uncanny, subliminal way that he wasn't there.

Scolding herself for being foolishly fanciful, Sorrel sketched a shrug and headed for the kitchen. 'Hello,' she said cheerfully, opening the door.

Penn dumped a casserole dish onto the bench before swivelling around, one hand pressed to her heart.

'Oh!' she exclaimed, then let out a huff of breath and smiled. 'Sorry, I get a bit jumpy when I'm alone. Lunch is ready—I've set it out buffet-style on the table in the family room, if that's all right with you. It's through here.' She bustled towards the hall.

'Great,' Sorrel said, following her and deducing that from now on she'd better knock whenever she arrived at Waimanu. 'How long has Luke being flying helicopters?'

'Oh, it must be four or five years—ever since he bought one.' The other woman pushed open a door and stood back to let Sorrel go first into the pleasant room in which she and Luke had eaten their breakfast. 'He wouldn't be able to manage without it. Running a big agricultural company means a lot of travelling, and of course he has a busy social life too.' She added with a guileless smile, 'He's going to some big film premiere tonight with his—his friend, Miss O'Neill.'

In spite of the sliver of dark emotion that stabbed Sorrel to the heart, she kept the mask of polite interest in place. 'Sounds fun,' she said noncommittally.

'I suppose you used to go to lots of them when you were modelling.'

'Quite a few.'

Another wide, ingenuous smile from the house-keeper. 'It must have been so exciting to have cameras flash at you and everybody watching you go in!'

'You get used to it. One of the good things about being a model,' Sorrel told her cheerfully, 'is that because you're there as decoration nobody expects you to have enough intelligence to string more than a couple of words together, so at least they don't ambush you with microphones.'

Penn looked startled. 'Well, yes, there's that, I suppose. By the way, Luke asked me to reassure you that you're welcome to stay here as long as you like, and of course if there's anything I can do to help you, you must let me know.'

'How very kind,' Sorrel murmured. 'As it happens, there is…'

An hour later she strode back to Parenga, carrying a bucket of cloths, scrubbers and various bottles of detergents. The housekeeper had handed them over with a polite smirk that indicated she didn't believe her unwelcome guest knew anything at all about housework.

'So I will show her,' Sorrel said between her teeth. 'And anyone else who thinks I'm just a useless ornament!'

Not that her afternoon of ferocious cleaning was really to show anyone that she wasn't a useless ornament; instead, she used the hard work to block out the violent jealousy that had needled her since the housekeeper told her why Luke had gone to Auckland. Scrubbing and mopping the kitchen and bathrooms kept her busy enough not to dwell obsessively on mental pictures of him with Mari O'Neill. In fact, she sometimes went for ten minutes without more than an occasional thought of them making love.

By the time she arrived back at Waimanu that evening she was grubby and hot, longing only to wash and then eat. Cleanliness came first, and when she finally came down the staircase after a long, luxurious bath, Penn was waiting at the foot of the stairs.

'Why don't you go into the sitting room?' the housekeeper suggested. 'I'll pour you a drink and serve dinner when you're ready. You must be exhausted.' She marched down to a door and opened it.

'I'm a little tired,' Sorrel admitted, curbing the impulse to point out that, although she wouldn't have been able to spend a day wielding a crowbar, she was neither fragile nor useless. Just inside the sitting room she stopped and said, 'I'm sure you're busy enough without having to bother about me. It seems a waste of your time to prepare meals when I can do it myself.'

'Luke wouldn't like that,' Penn stated, as though Luke's wishes were edicts engraved in stone. She met Sorrel's eyes with a movement of her lips that was less a smile than a challenge.

Why, if Mari O'Neill was still an important part of Luke's life, did Penn see Sorrel as a threat?

Possibly because a woman climbing the corporate ladder in Auckland didn't interfere with her position at Waimanu. More likely because the housekeeper liked Mari. That wouldn't be surprising; most people did.

Hell, even with her adolescent heart breaking, *Sorrel* had liked her!

'What would you care to drink?' the housekeeper asked in a tone verging on the proprietorial.

'Nothing, thank you,' Sorrel said collectedly, refusing to be irritated by the attempts to patronise her. 'I'll have dinner on a tray and then go up to my room.'

Penn looked taken aback. 'Oh, but—'

'Thank you,' Sorrel said firmly.

'If you're sure that's what you want?' the housekeeper said doubtfully.

'Certain.' Sorrel waited until the woman had left before looking around the opulent sitting room with its view of the river across a long terrace. Gracious and relaxing though it was, it didn't soothe her at all.

And neither did meditation later that evening. Years before, Sorrel had discovered meditation as a tool for serenity, but this time it failed her. After a frustrating twenty minutes spent visualising Luke with Mari in full Technicolor, she opened her eyes.

Loneliness punched her in the heart, driving her to her feet and across to the windows. Her best friend lived only an hour's drive away, but Emma and her husband, Kane Talbot, were in Canada with their delectable four-year-old daughter—Sorrel's goddaughter Cressy—and not due home for another three weeks. It would be great to live so near them…

She'd flown up to Vancouver to see them before she'd come on to New Zealand. It had been a bittersweet occasion; Emma was so happy with her gorgeous husband that Sorrel had to try hard not to envy her.

As for Cressy…

Sorrel leaned out and breathed in the cool, faintly saline air. An unknown scent—almost overpoweringly sweet—rose strongly from the garden below. It had been a real wrench to leave Cressy behind. Still, she'd see her again soon.

Sorrel bit her lip. Little Cressy was a darling, but she wanted her own children, she realised with something close to shock. OK, cuddling her goddaughter had probably set her biological clock ticking, but why did her childless state suddenly seem so poignant?

What was Luke doing right this moment?

'Oh, for heaven's sake!' she muttered, trying hard to banish Mari's voluptuous figure and her lovely, vital face from her brain.

Had Luke thought it was Mari he was kissing last night, until he'd woken sufficiently to realise who was in his arms?

Humiliation drained the colour from her skin.

Perhaps that was how it had begun, she reassured herself, but he'd known who she was when he'd touched her breast. And somehow she couldn't see Luke as a betrayer.

So whatever relationship he had with Mari had to be less than an affair. Or was she merely thinking wishfully, endowing him with virtues he didn't have?

She didn't know enough about Luke to be sure.

Her brooding gaze swept the garden below, taking in a froth of white along one border, a glimmer of silver through the trees where starlight was reflected from the water. A quick knock was a welcome interruption to her tormented thoughts.

'Sitting in the dark?' the housekeeper enquired brightly when Sorrel opened the door to her.

'Enjoying the view from the window.'

'It's beautiful, isn't it? Now, I've finished for the night,' Penn said, 'but before I go I thought I'd better tell you that the house has security all through it, so if you need anything from outside your room you should get it now, before I turn the alarms on.'

'I don't need anything,' Sorrel said quietly. 'Goodnight.' She closed the door with a sharp click.

Talk about a heavy-handed hint not to go wandering around!

Fuming, she went back to the window. If she leaned out a bit she could just see the roof of Parenga through the trees, dim in the gathering darkness.

Yesterday she'd arrived with such high hopes, expecting to build a new life here, only to find her plans crashing around her ears within the first twenty-four hours. She'd been confident Luke meant nothing to her; instead she'd taken one look at him and responded to his potent masculinity with the same shaken, helpless intensity as she had ten years ago.

Spending the first night in his arms had been a particularly nasty twist of fate. She'd burned with a forgotten, familiar need, her common sense driven like ashes before the wind in a firestorm of hungry sensation.

Just thinking about it fuelled an elemental longing so urgent she had to grit her teeth and clench her hands on the windowsill to stop them from shaking.

'Degrading,' she muttered. She drew back and turned around to look at the beautiful room. Something that had been teasing her popped into the forefront of her brain. Why hadn't Luke furnished any other bedrooms but his own and this one?

Perhaps because he was waiting for Mari to do it?

'Oh, stop it,' she muttered, heading into the bathroom. If twenty-four hours at Parenga had done this to her, how was she going to last out six months?

'Because you have to,' she said clearly, turning on the taps over the basin. 'And because Cynthia wanted you to.'

This obsession with Luke was just a hangover from adolescence, something she didn't want and couldn't afford—but something she could overcome with doses of common sense and will-power. She'd find salvation in cleaning and painting Parenga's shabby walls and woodwork; surely it wouldn't be too expensive, or difficult. Sorrel wasn't afraid of hard work, and nowadays—if television ads were to be believed—paint flowed onto walls by itself.

But what about exposing her heart in the process?

A chill of foreboding shivered through her.

Automatically going through her nightly routine, she wondered fretfully why Luke seemed to have taken up permanent residence in her—well, not in her heart, that was certain. She didn't love him, but oh, what he did to her hormones! It was unfair and unnerving and dangerous.

Other women smiled a little sentimentally when talking about their first love, then tied the memories in pastel scented ribbons and tucked them away for ever. Why hadn't it happened that way for her? She'd never managed to struggle free from the memory of one kiss.

One kiss! Hardly enough to build a lifetime of memories on. Yet her recollection glowed, still bright and unfaded, as though she'd never grown older than the girl of eighteen who'd loved Luke from afar. If she closed her eyes she could see the way he'd bent down to her, the glitter of blue in his grey eyes, his dark, suddenly taut face. She'd held her breath, waiting to be rejected.

Instead, his lips had touched her mouth so gently she'd barely felt it, yet she'd shuddered with delight.

'You're so lovely,' he said in a deep, gentle tone without lifting his head.

Entranced by the feel of his words against her sensitive skin, it took her a moment to register a kind of regret in his voice. He was going to stop.

No! Her height and the constant moves from school to school meant that this was Sorrel's first kiss; she had no idea what to do next, but she remembered films she had seen and shyly opened her lips, put one hand lightly, tentatively on his chest.

He froze, but beneath the heel of her hand his heartbeat ricocheted into a hard, pounding beat. Exultant, her hold on reality slipping fast, Sorrel wasn't expecting what followed. Luke made an odd raw noise in his throat and his mouth hardened on hers as his arms tightened around her, bringing her against a taut, almost aggressive body, lean and so big she was swamped by his assertive male strength.

But she melted against him, enchanted by new and thrilling sensations. He possessed himself of her mouth in a kiss that laid claim to everything female about her, and she yielded, submissive yet demanding her own surrender, her own power…

'Oh, yes, it was magnificent—soul-shattering, mind-bending, earth-shaking—but don't forget what happened next,' she reminded herself now, staring belligerently into the mirror. 'Let's see. He pulled away, just as he did last night, and he apologised—very abruptly, as though he hated you—and then said he'd never do it again.'

But it was the remembered note of self-contempt in his deep voice that haunted the gold-green eyes gazing back at her. He'd kissed her with a starving intensity that still sent shivers down her spine, yet he'd despised himself for it—just as he had last night.

She stiffened her jaw and turned away to dry her face.

Despise himself or not, however, he wanted her. So why not indulge in a wild affair and finally douse that consuming desire that had smouldered in her for so long? The realities of an affair—sex without commitment—would certainly strip those pretty ribbons from her memories and replace them with workaday string. No man could live up to the expectations she'd built of Luke.

The idea was seductively attractive, but even as her heart beat faster and colour scorched her skin she discarded it. An age-old feminine instinct warned her that taking Luke for a lover was *not* the way to root out the hold he had on her emotions. It would change her for ever.

Besides, the previous night had reinforced with cruel force that he felt nothing more for her than a crude, sexual hunger. She deserved better than that.

Yes, she had a life to make for herself, and Parenga was the first step. She'd find the strength to resist Luke's effect on her.

Probably she should be grateful that if he knew about it he'd wholeheartedly support her decision!

The morning after Luke flew out the road was cleared and the power switched back on, so Sorrel collected her provisions from the fridge at Waimanu, thanked Penn, and drove back to Parenga.

That afternoon she went into Kerikeri to replace the cleaning equipment she'd borrowed and liberate

Cynthia's furniture from the storage unit. The carriers piled it carefully in the garage. She hated to see it like that, a life reduced to a heap, but at least she was now saving the weekly rental. She needed that money.

Days passed in a blur. Sorrel scoured the inside of the house, then chose paint colours and bought the paint, working so hard that every night she fell into bed and slept dreamlessly without stirring.

The difficult part was actually getting to sleep; each night she lay for hours with memories of Luke's kisses burning through her with erotic intensity.

Now, more than a week after he'd left, Sorrel walked back in the dusk from a jaunt along the beach, realising with angry irritation that she'd spent every one of those days listening for the unmistakable sound of the helicopter.

'Get over him!' she commanded on a caustic note, bending to sniff the sweet, musky scent of the first gardenia bloom. Summer was rapidly ousting spring, bringing with it other flowers—brilliant vireya rhododendrons from the tropics and the first frilly, saturated scarlet hibiscus to blend with the bright buds of lilies and the bold blue of agapanthus.

Wincing at an ache in her back, she straightened up and surveyed her domain. She'd told the gardener she no longer needed him, and had resurrected Cynthia's elderly mower for the lawns, but the flowerbeds were still showing a lack of care.

'I'll get to you as soon as the house is in shape,' she promised.

Next week would be devoted to painting and polishing and a painful, judicious weeding out of the furniture her godmother had collected over a lifetime. Cynthia's magpie instincts had crowded every room in the house, and selling some of her treasures would bring in money to help pay for a replacement length of guttering and, if she was lucky, a few of the minor repairs needed.

'In the meantime,' Sorrel told Baggie as she put out his food and opened the back door a fraction so he could head out for his nightly inspection of the property, 'I'm going to have a bath and soak for at least half an hour.'

Ten minutes later she lowered herself gratefully into the bath, almost purring as the water, silky with a few drops of oil, lapped around her.

'Bliss,' she groaned, and leaned her head back, stretching out her arms along the cool sides of the old-fashioned tub and wallowing in the immeasurable comfort of scented water.

I'd better get out, she thought the second time she had to force her eyelids up.

She woke with a jolt to the sound of her name, shouted in a furious masculine voice. 'Sorrel! Sorrel, where the hell are you?'

'Here,' she croaked before she had time to think, blinking and reaching for her towel in the darkness.

'Where?'

Her mouth dried and she sat up. *Luke!* Her bones weighed her down so that when she tried to stand her legs refused to accept her weight. A startled cry broke from her lips as she slipped, falling back into the water with a splash.

'What—?'

Light blinded her.

He strode in, absorbed in one comprehensive glance the sight of her cowering in the bath with the wet towel held against her like a shield, and bent to pull out the plug. 'For God's sake, Sorrel, don't tell me you were idiotic enough to go to sleep in the bath!'

'I—yes,' she muttered, horrified by her foolishness.

'You could have drowned yourself!' Grim grey eyes took in her feeble attempts to hide behind the towel.

'Luke, go away, please.' She shivered and looked numbly down at her long bare legs revealed by the gurgling water.

'Get up.' When she didn't move he said tersely, 'You can't, can you?'

In one powerful, economical movement he leaned over, picked her up and set her on her feet on the bath-mat. Once more her treacherous legs collapsed, but as Luke's arms clamped around her something feverish stirred in the pit of her stomach, a primitive response, needle-sharp yet melting and honey-sweet.

She said, 'I'm making you wet—'

'Of all the stupid, reckless, carelessly irresponsible things to do,' he snarled. 'Damn it, Sorrel—'

He lifted her off her feet and strode out into the hall, with her positioned like a child—or a lover—in his arms.

Trembling with shock, she stiffened and fought the weakness that relished the heat from his body and its solid, feral strength.

'Put me down,' she said in a jerky voice, her heart beating crazily in her breast.

'You can't even stand up; what makes you think you'll be able to walk?'

He was right. Changing tack, she said, 'Not up-stairs—I'm sleeping in the maid's room at the back.'

After a second's hesitation, he moved steadily and surely through the darkened house. 'How long were you in that bath?' he demanded.

'I don't know—since dusk.'

'Over an hour.' His voice hardened even further. 'You need a keeper.'

'It won't happen again.' Thank heavens for the friendly night; he wouldn't be able to see anything more of her naked body than a pale blob in his arms.

His icy, ferocious anger engulfed her. 'It had better bloody not. Why are you sleeping downstairs?'

'It's more convenient.'

He elbowed the door open, switched on the light and took a couple of steps into the small room, swearing under his breath when he kicked the end of the double bed that took up most of it. A moment later she was on her feet, white-lipped and swaying.

Lean hands fastened onto her shoulders; ignoring her protest, he turned her to him, dark face closed against her as he began to rub her dry.

'I can do that,' she said thickly, clutching the towel around her.

'At the moment I feel more like shaking common sense into you than flinging you onto the bed and making wild, passionate love, believe me,' he said with satirical emphasis.

Gritting her teeth, she said, 'I can dry myself.'

'All right, show me.'

Her muscles were as floppy as jelly, and she was still paralysed with horror at what might have happened if Luke hadn't come in. Nevertheless, she wasn't going to let him dry her. She said raggedly, 'Get out, Luke!'

Baggie, who'd appeared from nowhere, wound himself around Luke's ankles. Ignoring the cat, Luke asked in a voice that sent frigid shivers scudding down her spine, 'Can you manage?'

'Of course I can,' she muttered, and began to dry her shivering skin.

'I'll make some tea,' he said curtly. 'Yell if you need help.'

Without looking at her he strode across the room and disappeared silently down the hall towards the kitchen.

Sorrel watched him go, then collapsed onto the side of the bed and finished drying herself.

When that was done, she looked at the jeans she'd been planning to wear and knew she wasn't going to be able to get into them. She had all the strength of a cooked noodle.

Forced into action by the thought of Luke coming for her, she got to her feet and staggered to the wardrobe, where she chose a long wrap-around skirt and a shell top, thankful that she didn't need to worry about a bra.

Even so it was a struggle, but she was decently covered and combing her hair when Lucas appeared in the doorway.

He scanned her face with a frigid, thin-lipped lack of compromise. 'How are you feeling?'

'Much better, thanks.' Sorrel's glance slipped past the wet patch across his shirt where he'd held her.

Avoiding his intent stare, she got up and walked with deliberate care towards him, encouraged by a spurt of adrenalin-induced energy. 'Perfectly normal, as you can see.'

He watched her narrowly, reluctantly appreciating her stubborn determination not to give in. She was steady enough on her feet, but he'd stay close by to make sure she didn't fall.

He stood back to let her through the door and caught a light fragrance—sweet, yet with a sultry undernote—

that stripped the years away as though they'd never happened. Cynthia had given her that perfume for her eighteenth birthday; perhaps, he thought, calling on cynicism to rescue him from a humiliating enslavement of the senses, she was wearing it because she knew of perfume's ability to lodge in the memory.

Face bare of cosmetics, hair pulled back in an untidy knot, shadows beneath her eyes, she looked heart-shakingly beautiful—even more beautiful than in that photograph of her naked in another man's arms, her lovely face lifted to his, her smile a slow, wondering invitation.

Savagely angry, Luke followed her down the hall, ready to catch her if she fell. She didn't, but she stumbled occasionally, once putting out a hand to brace herself against the wall.

In the kitchen she sat down at the table in the breakfast area, more colour in her face. 'I'm sorry,' she said unexpectedly.

'For almost killing yourself?' he asked, tamping down on his anger.

She nodded, her gold-green eyes avoiding his. 'Well, for being stupid. From now on I'll shower, or set an alarm.'

'I suppose it's no use asking you to come and stay at the homestead?'

'No.' She gave a swift little shudder. 'Believe me, falling asleep like that scared me. I won't do it again.'

She looked so fragile he wanted to drag her back to Waimanu and chain her to his wrist. He'd never forget the sight of her in the bath, unable to stand, unable even to think. If he'd been even a few minutes later she might well have drowned.

Frustrated, because he knew there was no way he

could make a direct order stick, he poured two mugs of tea and brought them to the table. 'You always were as obstinate as a chunk of granite,' he said bluntly as he sat down opposite her.

Sorrel laughed and picked up the mug he pushed across to her. 'It takes one chunk of granite to know another,' she said. Without looking at him she drank, managing not to wrinkle her nose at the overdose of sugar in the hot liquid.

'Finish it,' he said, judging her reaction too well. 'Why were you so tired? What have you been doing?'

Sorrel turned her head away from him, presenting her elegant profile. 'Sanding down the woodwork in the main bathroom.'

She was acutely conscious of that steady iron-grey gaze as he drank some of his own tea, watching her above the rim of the mug. It was an oddly intimate moment, made more so by the dark patch on his shirt. Shivery excitement replaced Sorrel's exhaustion. She said reluctantly, 'Do you want to put your shirt in the drier?'

'No, it's almost dry,' he said indifferently. 'What's going on? Penn tells me you borrowed cleaning things from her, and that you've been working solidly ever since I left. Trying to prove something, Sorrel?'

She examined the bottom of her cup. 'Why should I do that?'

'I don't know,' he said with cool calculation, burnished gaze fixed on her face. 'What exactly are your plans?'

She glanced away. 'If I decide to stay I'm seriously thinking of turning Parenga into a very upscale bed and breakfast.'

His eyes narrowed into slivers of molten metal. 'The

hell you are,' he said softly. He leaned back in his chair and surveyed her with chilling intensity. 'You'll need council permission.'

'I contacted them today,' she said levelly. 'The man I spoke to said he didn't anticipate any problems unless my neighbours object. Are you going to object, Luke?'

CHAPTER SEVEN

'I'LL need more information before I make a decision,' Luke said drily. 'Drink your tea, and then come and have dinner with me at Waimanu. You can tell me about it there.'

It wasn't a threat—he even smiled faintly at her as he made the invitation—but Sorrel detected a note in his words that sent prickles of unease down her spine. He might not be able to prevent her from setting up Parenga as a bed and breakfast, but he wielded a lot of power in the North; he could delay the process and make it much more expensive.

So she agreed with a certain amount of reserve. 'All right. I'll just get changed.'

His brows lifted as he surveyed her. 'You look fine.' And after a pause, in a harder voice, 'Exquisite.'

Did he think she planned to seduce him into accepting her plan? Resentment pulsed through her, burnishing her skin and restoring her strength. 'Thank you,' she said with composure. 'Did you enjoy the film premiere?'

The shutters slammed down, leaving his handsome face expressionless. 'Very much. Mari sent her regards, by the way.'

'That's kind of her.' It sounded so stiff that she drank more tea, striving to come up with some light—but sophisticated—remark. Her brain remaining obstinately blank, she finished the repulsively sweet tea and stood up.

'How do you feel?' Luke asked, rising with her.

'Slightly odd,' she admitted. 'A bit floaty, but that might be because it's a couple of hours after my usual dinnertime. Better than I deserve to feel.'

'Indeed.' The crisp intonation told her he was still angry. 'Next time lock the door to the house. I walked straight in.'

An undercurrent in his voice sent her heartbeat soaring, reminding her of the moments when he'd held her naked in his arms.

And not shown the slightest interest in her beyond a surprising unleashed fury at her stupidity. 'Baggie likes to go for an evening prowl after his night meal,' she said, striving for an objective tone instead of infuriating defensiveness. 'Besides, if I hadn't left it open you wouldn't have been able to come in.' And she might have drowned.

Luke paused, hiding his thoughts behind that impassive face and those hooded eyes. 'Your car's there, so I knew you were home. If you hadn't answered I'd have hammered on the door until you did. Next time you go into town buy a cat door. It's not safe, even here, to leave doors unlocked. I've lost cattle to rustlers, and there have been farm burglaries in the district.'

She said sombrely, 'So there's no safe place any more?'

'Nowhere in this world,' he said, adding with brutal realism, 'But then, there never has been.'

Sorrel was more afraid of the heady combination of arousal and anticipation in her blood than she was of any criminal. Near Luke she came alive, as though she'd spent her previous life sleepwalking.

Stay cool, she told herself. He doesn't want to want

you, and you aren't going to scratch his itch just for the excitement of it.

He's more than you can handle.

In the big sitting room at Waimanu he waited until she was sitting down before measuring her with a glance as sharp as a scalpel, a glance that clashed with his smooth tone. 'Wine? There's a rather nice *sauvignon blanc* here from Marlborough.'

'I'd love some, thank you.'

He brought across a glass of pale golden liquid that hinted at summer, before pouring himself a short whisky with water. With it untasted in his hand, he sat down in the largest armchair opposite her. 'Now, tell me why you've decided to set up in the hospitality business.'

She lifted the fragile barrier of the glass against him and sipped, letting the chilled liquid slide down her throat. 'I have to do something. I like entertaining and I'm a good cook.'

'It's a huge change from the high life.'

'The high life as in nursing my father?' She didn't try to hide the satirical inflection in her words.

Thick dark lashes drooped over gunmetal eyes. 'You were a very dutiful daughter,' he observed neutrally.

She shrugged. 'He needed me.'

'I admire you for taking care of him, but I still can't see why you want to set up as a glorified motel-keeper. Why don't you go back to modelling?'

'Once you drop out it's pretty hard to get back in,' she said lightly, 'especially at my age. There are lots of gorgeous sixteen- and seventeen-year-old girls out there, who don't need much in the way of airbrushing to look perfect.' She smiled with cynical understanding. 'And they're much cheaper.'

A harsh scream from outside startled her. 'What—? Oh, a pukeko,' she said on an uneven little laugh. 'Until I came back I'd forgotten what a noise they can make, and they still startle me.' The blue swamp hens with their scarlet legs and Roman beaks were a common sight on the riverbank.

'So you've given it all away,' Luke said reflectively, although his regard was keen and perceptive. 'It must have been difficult to turn your back on success.'

She swallowed some more wine, fragrant and delicious. Half a glass, she decided later, wasn't enough to explain her decision to say, 'My father wasn't getting anywhere in hospital. As long as I was there I could bully him into therapy, but if I left him he refused to do anything. Besides, it was no great sacrifice. Modelling wasn't really my choice as a career.'

He lifted black brows in a movement both ironic and disbelieving. 'So you said before. Why do it if you disliked it?'

Of course *he* wouldn't have. Luke made his own decisions and followed them through no matter how much it cost him. She got to her feet and walked across to the window. The outside lights had been left on and in their gentle glow the garden assumed a beauty and mystery that caught at her heart.

Although it had been a cloudy, humid day, the sky had cleared to reveal the curl of a new moon, a sliver of pearl in a sky of velvet, its light softly polishing the waters of the river.

She said, 'When I was thirteen I started to grow. In six months I shot up from being small and thin and redheaded to being tall and thin and redheaded, far more than head and shoulders above everyone else in the classroom. I was teased unmercifully until I took that modelling course and won the competition. And then suddenly it was a wonderful thing to be tall, to have red hair; I was photographed and flattered and sought-after, welcomed everywhere I went.'

'You were welcomed here,' he said crisply.

'As an appendage to Cynthia, yes.' She leaned forward to watch a pukeko strut across the lawn, arrogantly striding out of the pool of light into darkness.

Choosing her words carefully, she continued, 'It was intoxicating stuff, and I'd be lying if I said I didn't enjoy it, but I soon found that modelling itself wasn't satisfying. I liked parts of it—working with intensely creative people enriched me enormously—but most of it I just…endured.'

Not like her father, who'd loved the stimulation, the fascinating, larger-than-life people inhabiting that world, the full-on intensity of it.

Yet even that hadn't been enough for him; he'd craved more.

'But the money was too good to turn down?' Luke said levelly.

She flicked a sideways glance at him. 'Yes,' she said in a muted voice. 'That too.'

Burnished eyes scanned her with cool appraisal. 'You're looking a bit fragile. Come and sit down again.'

Sorrel obeyed, gazing into the fragrant depths of her glass and wondering what had driven her to confide in him.

Certainly not the hope that he'd understand!

He said, 'So you've always seen yourself as an outsider?'

Her head came up swiftly. Startled at his perception, she shook her hair across her face and hid behind it as she sipped some of the wine. 'I suppose so, although I hadn't actually put it in words. Every other kid had a mother, to start off with. We moved around a lot, so I was always the new pupil at school. Then I grew into the freak who towered over her classmates.'

'And finally the unattainable trophy woman smiling from the pages of expensive magazines,' he finished blandly.

She nodded. 'Don't think I'm wallowing in self-pity, because I'm not. I've had more luck than most women my age, and I don't regret any of it.'

'But?'

Lips tilting wryly, she said, 'I suppose I feel that I don't know who I am, where I belong.'

'So you've come back to find yourself?'

The mocking question set her temper alight. 'Don't put words in my mouth. And it's easy to scoff when you've always known who you were—as the heir to Waimanu, with the prestige of being a Hardcastle, your position has always been secure.'

'We do share some experiences,' he said, his eyes hard as they measured her face. 'Mothers who abandoned us—'

She made an instinctive sound of rejection but he went on ruthlessly, 'To a child, death is abandonment. And we both had fathers who were—unsatisfactory.'

'What do you mean?'

'My father was a fool over women. Yours had itchy feet and couldn't—or wouldn't—provide you with any sense of stability, of belonging.'

'He did his best for me,' she flared, refusing to accept his dispassionate summation.

'When it didn't clash with his aspirations,' Luke said inflexibly. 'My father submerged himself to please his wives, but they left him anyway.'

She said, 'So you don't trust women.'

'That's too easy and pat.' His jaw tightened. 'Do you believe that if you love someone they'll abandon you?'

'Of course I don't,' she said, shrugging to hide an uncomfortable shiver. If he didn't trust his father's taste in women, then he didn't trust her. Sorrel shared fine bones and height and a coppery mass of hair with the woman the district called The Wicked Stepmother— always pronounced in capitals. Cherie Hardcastle had been about four inches shorter, but the superficial resemblance had been startling.

He stood up. 'Dinner must be ready—bring your wine, you can finish it at the table.'

Over an excellent meal they discussed books and music and television programmes. Slow-burning excitement lent brilliance to Sorrel's eyes, sharpened her wits and lifted her spirits.

Halfway through the main course a knock on the door surprised them both. Frowning, Luke looked across the room. 'Come in.'

The housekeeper said, 'Sorry, Luke, but Miss O'Neill's on the phone. She says it's important.'

'Thank you,' Luke said. He waited until Penn had closed the door before asking with cool courtesy, 'Do you mind if I take this call?'

'Of course not.'

Sorrel watched him go before forcing herself to eat a mouthful of beans, followed in due course by a small amount of sesame steak—tender and delicious before, tasteless now.

Just as well Mari had rung, because Sorrel had fallen

into a trap she'd set herself. Stimulated by Luke's incisive intelligence and his wide knowledge, she'd forgotten about the woman who was clearly still very much a part of his life.

He was like a drug, fascinating yet addictive—so dangerous that once in the bloodstream it could never be exorcised.

Panic clawed her as she realised for the first time how like her father she was, how close she was to losing everything he'd lost—self-respect, integrity, peace of mind—in a reckless, risk-filled fixation on something she'd never be able to reach.

No, she thought desperately. Unlike her father, she knew when to pull away.

Right now.

No more dinners, no more matching wits with Luke, no more lazy surrender to a need she didn't dare appease.

He wasn't away long, and although his expression remained inscrutable some subliminal part of Sorrel recognised a buried anger behind his detachment.

'Sorry,' he said calmly.

'Not to worry.' Sorrel cut off another slice of steak and chewed it with dogged perseverance. Did Mari ring him every night?

And this slash of dark emotion was *not* jealousy. Jealousy implied some prior rights, and she had none.

She began to talk about a magazine article she'd read.

Eventually dinner ended; she drank a cup of tea before producing a yawn. 'Time for me to go, I think,' she said with her most charming smile. 'I know we haven't discussed my plans yet, but I'm suddenly very tired.'

Luke stood immediately, keen eyes scrutinising her face for an intent moment. 'Yes, you look as though you could do with an early night,' he said crisply.

Outside the crescent moon had long set. Once in Luke's car Sorrel sat in silence, watching the competent movements of his hands on the wheel.

Just over the bridge he stopped the vehicle. 'Did you feel that?'

'A slight shudder? Something wrong with the car, do you think?'

After grabbing a torch he opened the door and got out. 'It's probably nothing.'

Sorrel emerged from her side. 'If it's not the car, what would it be?'

'That's what I want to find out.' Luke directed a hard-edged beam of light towards the bridge.

The warm night was heavy with the scents of early summer—the tang of the sea, sensuous perfume from Cynthia's climbing roses, the green lushness of growth and fecundity. A poignant, aching hunger twined its way through Sorrel, feeding on repressed emotions, deliberately forgotten memories.

Straightening defiantly, she walked around to join him as he played the torch across the wooden bridge decking. 'Is it the bridge?'

Say no, she pleaded silently. Tell me the bridge is fine…

'I can't see anything,' he said, turning back. 'It may just have been a stone lying the wrong way.'

She nodded, hoping sickly that he was right. Bridge repairs had to mean serious money—money she didn't have.

Luke said, 'I'll look at it tomorrow morning.'

Be firm she told herself. You've made your decision; carry through on it. 'You don't need to—I can.'

'Do you know anything about bridges?' He sounded amused.

'I could probably tell whether there was something wrong with it,' she parried, climbing back into the car.

He joined her and tossed the torch into the back seat. 'Independence is a fine thing, but it won't take me long to check it out.'

While he put the car into gear Sorrel chewed her lip and gazed up the drive. Of course he was right; what did she know about the structure of bridges?

Allowing a neighbourly act on his part wouldn't feed her addiction.

Outside the house, wrapped by the perfume of a thousand flowers on the mock orange, Luke said, 'Is the back door locked?'

'Yes, I made sure before we left.' When he held out his hand for the key she said lightly, 'I can open my own door.'

He stepped back with an ironic inclination of his head, and she inserted the key and pushed the door open, switching on the inside light before she turned to face him.

'Thank you for a lovely evening,' she said inanely, trying to sound formal and fully in control as she stared at his throat. She'd probably have coped if she hadn't glanced up.

The light revealed a face dark and drawn, intent and angular. 'No,' Sorrel whispered, but she didn't move. She couldn't.

'Why not?' A jagged edge of raw desire in his voice unmasked a hunger that called to the wildness in her. Yet he didn't touch her.

Her lips shaped his name and he reached out and traced it with a long forefinger on her mouth. Need flowered, violently insistent, sweet as comb honey, ruthless as a flooded river.

Then he cupped her chin, tilting her face so that she was exposed to his devouring gaze. She almost cried out at the blaze of his eyes, the heated, merciless sensuality that prowled their pewter depths.

Words thick and impeded, she said, 'I don't poach.' Just as Mari had said all those years ago.

'I've made no commitment to anyone.' He spoke as though it wasn't important, as though he could think of nothing but the hunger that linked them both with unbreakable bonds. 'And there's no one for you.' It wasn't a question.

'No.' There never had been. Not like this.

He kissed the word away, and with it fled all the shoddy conjuring tricks she'd played on her mind to convince herself she didn't love him.

Because this wasn't some obsession, an addiction she could fight.

She had learned to love Luke when she'd been too young to know what love was, and before she'd understood the daunting force of sexual passion.

When he'd kissed her she'd discovered that desire hit like an earthquake, ferocious in its force, mindless and inevitable, changing everything. Now, mouth crushed beneath his and the heated fumes of carnal longing shutting down reason and logic, she realised with a stripped, stark flash of insight that, like her father, she would only ever love once.

Here, in Luke's arms, was her true home.

He lifted his head and said harshly, 'Tell me now if you still feel weak.'

'No.'

Her doubts, her fears, the reasons she'd refused to accept this hopeless love, still echoed around her brain. But although she knew she was courting heartache she craved her moment of glory.

Luke picked her up and walked through the door, kicking it closed behind them. Safe against him as he navigated the dark house with sure confidence, Sorrel turned her face into his throat, inhaling the faint, potent scent that was his alone.

His heart slammed into her side, gaining speed when she kissed his throat and then delicately licked the skin. He tasted of Luke—warm, sexual, all male. All hers. Exulting, she murmured his name in a voice she didn't recognise, slow and husky and sensuous, letting her lips linger against his skin.

Old fantasies flared in her mind, to be swamped by the reality of this—the quiet house, the heat from Luke's body, the careless, casual strength that supported her and surrounded her.

In the pit of her stomach, racing through her veins, exploding from cell to cell, the wildness inside her began to build, singing a song as ancient as Eve. Fingertips tingling, she traced the strong framework of his face, the lines of each brow and the sweep of an autocratic cheekbone. She touched him in the small, intimate ways of a lover, testing the smooth skin of his forehead, the roughened silk of his shaved cheek, the heat of his mouth.

Without faltering he bent his head and kissed her fiercely, then swung her down onto the bed.

The bedside lamp bloomed, casting a gentle pool of light over the bed. Pulses pounding, Sorrel lifted weighted eyelids and looked through her lashes into the hard, leashed danger of Luke's face.

For a moment her heart failed her, but caution was vaporised by the turbulent blue-grey depths of his eyes. He wanted her as no other man had, she realised with fierce delight. His unchained, elemental desire melted every defence. Lifting her hand, she followed the outline of his lips, and smiled.

Sultry, beckoning, that smile sent Luke's blood pressure through the ceiling. The night she'd spent sleeping in his arms had cracked his defences, sensitising him to the satin feel of her, the graceful warmth of limbs and breasts and hips.

Since then he'd caught himself listening for her laugh and the throaty, sensuous catch in her voice, watching the rich fall of red-brown hair, the sheen of ivory skin, the slow, radiant promise of her smile. Her sheer physical perfection had lodged in his brain until hunger had driven every logical thought before it, like clouds streaming ahead of a cyclone.

Why Sorrel? He'd enjoyed other beautiful women— and not just in bed. Most of his lovers were still friends. He could never be friendly with Sorrel, he thought grimly as he watched her on the bed, lovely face turned up to him in tantalising surrender. Perhaps he was a true son of his father—a fool about this woman.

But he had enough control not to surrender everything. Although she knew how her fine-boned, delicately sexy body affected men, making them wonder if they'd be the lucky one to coax her cool beauty into flames, she'd never learn that she was the only woman who could shatter his control.

He bitterly resented—even feared—her power; he'd

despised himself for not being able to ignore it and until a few minutes ago he'd been certain he could resist her.

But now to hell with restraint and self-sufficiency and everything else he'd lived his life by. He wanted Sorrel like he wanted to breathe. No—more than he wanted to breathe.

And this time nothing, not even his own defeat, was going to stop him.

'What are you thinking?' she asked huskily.

His mouth compressed, then relaxed into a sardonic smile. 'That I should have known this was inevitable.'

The abrasive cadence in his voice quickened a primal need. Shivering, she whispered, 'For both of us?'

'Yes.'

Her mouth softened. 'You are so beautiful,' she said on a sigh.

He laughed and came down beside her, sliding an arm beneath her head and turning her face towards his. 'Those are my words,' he said ambiguously. 'Beautiful beyond bearing. Beautiful enough to fog a man's mind, to drive his dreams at night and haunt him by day. More beautiful than any fantasy could be...'

For a long, taut second he looked into her eyes. Her stomach clenched. He was demanding complete capitulation, yet she couldn't read anything except desire in the iron-grey glitter of his eyes.

It didn't matter. *It didn't matter.* She loved him whatever he felt for her. When his name sighed out through her lips she heard her surrender in it, mingled with the longing that had been building for half her life.

And then he kissed her, and again Sorrel discovered what real passion felt like.

It was fire in her fingertips as she curved her hands around his face, fire in the masculine mouth that took hers and made it his, fire in the way he slipped the little shell top over her shoulders and bent his head to her breast.

She arched into his mouth, into the lean hand that cupped the slight mound, into his body, fierce and hot and urgent against her. That perilous, primitive fire leapt from her to him and back again, arrowing from the budding aureole of her breast to the sensitive inner passage that clamoured for him.

She pulled at the buttons on his shirt, wrenching them free so that she could feel the slow flex and play of his long muscles beneath his sleek skin, the sheer male strength of him calling to everything that was female in her.

Luke laughed under his breath. 'What do you want?'

'This.' Again she curved into his hard body, shuddering as she felt his involuntary response.

'Is that all?' He kissed her again until she was mad for the embrace his deep, deep kisses imitated.

Arms tight around his back, Sorrel curved once more into him, an unspoken plea catching in the back of her throat. 'I want you,' she said when she could speak.

'Everything?'

She bit his earlobe. 'Everything.' It was a vow.

'Just as well,' he said, thrusting against her. 'Because that's what I want from you—everything. All you can give me. All that you are.'

Held against his big, taut body, Sorrel gazed up, mouth drying when she realised the iron-grey irises of his eyes had been swallowed by smouldering blue.

There would, she knew, be no going back. Once she made love with Luke, no other man would do.

She smiled and kissed the hard perfection of his lips. Who cared? She'd never want any other man.

'All that I can give you,' she said into his mouth. 'All that I am.'

His arms contracted, and for the first time she felt the full force of his strength. They relaxed immediately. 'I'm sorry,' he said harshly. 'I won't hurt you.'

'I know.'

He kissed her with a heart-shaking blend of tenderness and desire, but the layers of fabric between them had become intolerable. She groaned into his mouth, and he found the fastening of her skirt as she found his trousers.

'Not yet,' he said, his voice deliberate yet raw. 'Let me.'

He stripped the skirt and shell top and the fragile pair of briefs from her, and began to kiss her slender, naked body, taking his time, dazzling her with his expertise and his knowledge of all the pleasure points in a woman's body. She'd had no idea that a man's mouth and hands could be so ruthlessly tender, or that each caress, each kiss, could pierce her body with a hungry rapture.

'I don't break,' he said quietly.

Sorrel blinked. 'I didn't—' she said in a dazed voice.

He knew, of course. He knew that she had never experienced anything like this deliberate, purposeful seduction.

And he must have guessed that she'd never responded like this before, with an untamed sensuousness that would have shocked her only a few weeks ago.

She turned her head into his chest and kissed the hot swell of muscle there, let her hands roam wherever they wanted to, skin against skin in a world that had narrowed down to this room, this bed, this man.

Still Luke continued his erotic voyage of discovery,

using skills she'd never heard of to summon pleasure, until eventually her whole body screamed for satisfaction. She said his name again, almost unable to hear her own voice above the jarring crash of her heartbeat in her ears.

Then, moving with silent speed and grace, he removed the rest of his clothes. He stood a moment by the bed, feasting his eyes on her.

Aching with keen-edged need, Sorrel leaned back against the pillows, committing to memory the powerful bone structure, the muscles earned by years of brutal physical work, the sleek, richly tanned skin…

Words trembled on her lips, but she bit them back. He didn't want to know that she loved him. So she leaned over and kissed the arrogant jut of one hip, letting her mouth linger until he said, 'Sorrel,' and came down beside her, pulling her down into his arms.

For a few precious seconds just lying half beneath him was enough, but soon she wanted more than this pressure from shoulder to thighs, the heat of his loins hard against hers.

'Please,' she whispered.

Luke lifted himself slightly, but Sorrel slid her arms around his shoulders to pull him back. 'Wait,' he said curtly, and she waited while he dealt with the condom he'd put on the table.

That done, he kissed her again, and this time he pushed slowly into her.

Sorrel's breath locked in her chest; she stared up into eyes as blue as exploding stars. He was uncomfortably big so she widened her legs, and when she'd opened herself to him he pushed home in a single, forceful movement.

He froze at her choked cry and began to withdraw,

but she clamped tight interior muscles and refused to allow it, claiming him as he had claimed her.

'God!' he said harshly, and kissed her deeply, holding her captive with his mouth until she relaxed. He withdrew and found her again, setting up a rhythm of discovery that echoed the patterns of her life.

Her hands slid lower, past his waist, to the flexing muscles of his buttocks, holding him against her. Sensation shuddered through her, wild and sweet and hot. She adjusted to his possession, carried further and further into a realm she'd only ever heard of before.

Higher and higher he took her, until the swirling waves of sensation coalesced into ecstasy and she came apart in his arms, pitched into a universe where the only thing that registered was a rapture beyond bearing.

He followed her there, face dark with intolerable ecstasy, his big body rigid as he poured himself into her.

Still in thrall to the aftershocks of her overpowering orgasm, she realised eventually that she was crying. Horrified, she tried to stop the silent tears, but they kept coming.

'Sorrel,' Luke rasped, turning onto his side with her still in his arms, 'did I hurt you?'

'No.' She wept harder.

He held her against his wide, bare shoulder. 'So what's going on?' His voice rumbled against her cheek.

'I don't know,' she whispered, wiping the tears away with the heel of her hand. She couldn't tell him that she'd never experienced anything like that before. Somehow he'd ripped her soul from her body and made it his.

'You're tired,' he said, smoothing the tumbled silk of her hair back from her face. 'Go to sleep.'

She wanted to stay awake, but almost instantly she sank into slumber. And Luke lay there with her lax, slender body draped across him and stared bleakly into the darkness.

CHAPTER EIGHT

SORREL woke to morning light pouring across her face and an importunate Baggie calling crossly from the doorway.

'OK, OK, give me time!' She stretched sensuously, wondering idly where her incredible sense of well-being came from.

And then she turned over and opened her eyes. There, on the pillow beside her, was the indentation made by Luke's head.

'Oh no,' she whispered, chilled to her bones. 'You crazy woman—how *could* you?'

Last night she'd decided to protect herself against Luke—then immediately surrendered with insulting, humiliating speed to his kisses, not even making a pretence at resistance.

Idiot! Fool! Ever since she'd come back she and Luke had fought a tense emotional duel; falling in love with him in adolescence had probably been inevitable, but making love with him at twenty-eight was an act of madness.

Groaning, she rolled over and buried her face in her pillow. She hated her weakness, the susceptibility that drowned out the sensible promptings of her brain in a flood of mindless fire. Was this how her father had felt when faced with the urge to gamble?

'Oh, Dad,' she whispered, 'I wish I'd realised how easy it is to give in.'

Unfortunately she couldn't hide in bed for the rest

of the day, however much she wanted to. She sat up and stared around the room, averting her eyes from the clothes she'd discarded so swiftly and thoughtlessly the previous night. Her mouth trembled. She'd never sleep in this bed again, come into this room again, without remembering her passionate, unrestrained response to Luke; his dominating presence would always haunt her.

Gripped by a cowardly impulse to run as far and as fast as she could, she eased herself out of the bed and shrugged into her robe.

No, she wasn't going to decamp, however tempting the idea. That had been her father's response; if she followed his example she might never be able to overcome this sensual enslavement. Facing it, dealing with it, was the only way she'd conquer it.

Besides, Cynthia had wanted her to stay in the house for six months, and she'd do that for her godmother, whatever the cost. Last night she'd reneged on her vow; all the more reason to stick to this decision.

'All right,' she said grimly, to a still yowling Baggie, 'what's done is done. Now I have to learn to live with my own stupidity and make sure I never repeat it.'

Having changed the linen on the bed and set the washing machine going, she was sanding down the skirting boards in the main bedroom when she heard Luke's car turn into the drive. It stopped on the other side of the bridge.

She bit her lip, her heart thudding with a kind of terrified excitement, and continued working. About ten minutes later he knocked on the front door.

Sorrel took a deep, shaking breath and went down to meet him.

He didn't look any different. Tall, dark, inflexible, his mouth a thin line, he said abruptly, 'It looks as though the last flood loosened the decking on the bridge.'

For a moment she couldn't think of what to say. 'I see.'

He said, 'I'll call a firm in Whangarei to fix it.'

'No—I'll do it.' At least while she was worrying about this she wasn't thinking about those maddened hours in his arms—well, not much.

'Sorrel, I know you're perfectly capable of doing it,' he said between his teeth, 'but I know this man. He's built a couple of bridges for me and repaired others. If I contact him he will give your job priority. And you need it done quickly—it's dangerous as it is. You'll also need to put a sign at the entrance to make sure no one else drives across it.'

She said quietly, 'Before I make any decisions I need a rough idea of how much it will cost.'

'Is that a problem?' He scrutinised her face with narrowed, intent eyes.

Her mouth folded into an obstinate line. 'I'm not stupid; I won't give a firm freedom to do what they like without an estimate first.'

Silence hummed between them—taut, filled with unspoken words. Sorrel sensed the swift, ruthless working of Luke's mind, and thought wearily that she should have shut up. But he couldn't have possibly heard anything about her father—she'd worked hard to prevent any gossip.

'Surely,' he said, in a voice that slashed her skin like a whip, 'you haven't let the entire, obscene amount of money you earned parading that glorious body slip through your fingers?'

She gasped. Mind completely blank, she looked into

eyes as cold and pitiless as granite. Inside she began to shake.

'Has it all gone, Sorrel?' he asked with merciless determination.

'It's vulgar to talk about money,' she parried, 'especially other people's. Have you any idea how much repairs might cost?'

He paused, then gave her a figure.

The hollowness in her stomach expanded, but she braced herself to meet his unsparing gaze with a limpid one of her own. 'I see,' she said.

Something in the way she said it—perhaps a note of panic—solidified Luke's barely formed suspicion into certainty. Knowing he was jumping to conclusions, he asked evenly, 'What did you spend it on, Sorrel? Cocaine? I believe it's the drug of choice amongst models nowadays.'

Disgust darkened her eyes as she returned with icy precision, 'You've been reading too many tabloids. I don't do drugs—never have.'

'So what did it go on?'

She stared straight at him, the fine-boned allure of her beautiful face replaced by open challenge. 'Bad investments.'

Luke was a man who followed his hunches, and so far they'd never let him down. She was lying.

He seized her chin between thumb and forefinger and tilted it, forcing her to meet his gaze. Deliberately, she lifted her lashes to uncover golden-green eyes, eyes that could turn overnight from smouldering passion to cool dismissal...

Flesh still hot with the remembered taste of her sultry mouth, he knew that beneath that beautiful, sexy mask, within the body that had given him ecstasy, hid a lying heart.

Did she, like his stepmother, see the owner of Waimanu as a source of ready cash? Had she come back to Parenga to see if that old, violent enchantment still had any life in it?

Fighting down a black rage, he forced himself to think dispassionately. It made sense. If she'd lost her money and been unable to take up her career again after the years spent looking after her father, then why not look around for some way of replacing that enviable lifestyle? A rich man...

And if she'd faked that passion last night it was just as well he'd found out immediately, before any damage was done.

He dropped her chin as though the silky skin burned his fingers and surveyed her with eyes as cold and keen as the blade of a sword. 'Gambling, Sorrel?'

'Go to hell,' she said with cool composure, but he saw the shock in her face, in her voice.

Yes, she'd wondered whether raking through old embers would start another fire, one big enough to keep her warm and secure for the rest of her life.

His mouth hardened into a smile as frigid as the polar wind. 'You gambled on the wrong man,' he told her. 'I learnt the lessons my father never did—look carefully at beautiful women when they offer themselves to you. Usually it's because they want something, and the something is usually money.'

For some reason she almost looked relieved, but the fleeting expression was instantly replaced by scepticism. 'You can't possibly believe that your only appeal to women is your money!'

He said contemptuously, 'Looks are important in

lovers and playthings, but they count for nothing when it comes to the serious business of lining pockets. My stepmother would have married my father if he'd been the ugliest man on earth.'

'How do you know?' Sorrel demanded, suddenly angry. 'An onlooker never understands the truth in a marriage.'

His eyes were cold, so cold she shivered. 'I understand that within six months of their marriage she tried to seduce me.'

Horrified, Sorrel stared at him. She read the truth in his relentless expression, heard it in his flat voice.

'Yes,' he said. 'I know what greed looks like in a woman—and desperation. Tell me, why did you sleep with me last night?'

'Not to line my pockets,' she retorted, ashamed and humiliated. 'And not because I was desperate either, believe me.'

'So why?'

Hands clenched at her sides, she took a step closer. 'To scratch an itch,' she hurled at him, hiding the pain that tore her apart with assumed hauteur. 'A ten-year-old itch. And now that I've dealt with it, that's an end to it.'

His eyes blazed. 'It's never that simple,' he said in a low, savage voice, and kissed her, imprisoning her against him as he plundered her mouth, stamping a claim on her that had nothing to do with desire and everything to do with angry possession.

Sorrel tried to fight him off, but the fire that roared through her overwhelmed any sensible decisions, all the promises she'd made for the future, and she kissed him back.

And somehow, even though she knew Luke intended

that kiss to be an assault, it changed. They kissed like lovers parting for a long time—like lovers who knew they would never meet again…

Tears sprang into her eyes, ached through her heart, because they were saying goodbye.

Slowly he released her, slowly straightened. She saw thin streaks of colour across his high cheekbones and knew that he was furious with himself for succumbing to temptation.

Anguish clamped her in a shroud of darkness. It took every last shred of strength to jut her chin in quick arrogance and step back. 'Goodbye, Luke,' she said with as much finality as she could manage. 'I'd be grateful if you'd drop the name of that bridge firm into the letterbox.'

He swung on his heel and walked out. She stood shaking, her hands clenched at her sides, fighting the need to run after him and tell him that he was wrong, that she loved him, that the intervening years hadn't been enough to break the link between them.

But he wouldn't believe her. And although it hurt that he should believe her to be tarred by the same brush as his stepmother, she thought now that she could see why. A young boy, unsure of himself and loving his father, having to fight off his father's new wife— oh, she thought viciously, there was enough trauma in that to mark him for life.

The sound of her car engine brought her out of her trance. She raced across to the window and saw it heading down the drive. Of course—she'd left the keys in it. She pressed her knuckles to her mouth, stifling the cry that longed to escape, and watched with hot, dry eyes as Luke drove slowly across the bridge and parked on the verge just inside the entrance.

He didn't look back. She saw him toss the keys into the letterbox, swing into his Land Rover and drive away.

'Go and get the keys,' she told herself brutally. 'You can cry later. You've got work to do and decisions to make.'

The bridge seemed firm when she walked over it, so presumably it was safe enough for pedestrians. But if she was going to open a bed and breakfast she'd have to find the money for repairs. Guests wouldn't want to carry their suitcases in from the road.

She went up to the main bedroom and began on the skirting boards again, finding some relief in the monotonous rhythm.

It was late when she forced herself into bed, and she was exhausted, but for hours she lay staring bleakly into the warm summer night while vivid images played and replayed through her treacherous mind.

In a morning heavy with the scent of sun and rain and growing greenery, she walked over Luke's land to the beach and tried to forget everything in a brisk run along the sand to the mouth of the river. It didn't work—but then years of pretence hadn't worked either.

'It seems Dad bequeathed me his addictive personality,' she told Baggie bleakly. 'No, idiot cat, don't go near the river—it's too clear for eels, and if you fall in there you'll get washed out to sea!'

For once the cat obeyed her and they turned for home. At the entrance Sorrel looked in the letterbox and found an envelope with her name on it in Luke's strong handwriting.

Heart skipping a beat, she ripped it open and read the name and telephone number of the bridge-builder. She wasn't surprised later, when she rang and the woman who answered the telephone told her she'd already pencilled in a date for a check and an estimate.

Just like a dentist, Sorrel thought wearily. And Luke had made the appointment.

The engineer turned up a couple days later, after a night when Sorrel had at last managed to snatch a few hours' sleep and so was feeling marginally human. Young, redheaded and confident, he was all business, although she recognised the admiring appraisal in his eyes.

After poking around the bridge for an hour or so, he knocked on the door of the house.

'How did it go?' Sorrel asked, hiding her concern with a smile.

'Not good, I'm afraid. Come on down and have a look—I can explain it better if I show you.'

Luke was right—the flood had managed to loosen the decking from the beams.

'Mind you,' the engineer said cheerfully, 'it needed replacing anyway.' He kicked a loose board. 'See? That's pretty close to disintegration.'

'What about the beams?' she asked, bending to survey the steel underpinning to the deck.

'No problems there.' He grinned at her.

'That's a relief. Can you give me a rough estimate of the cost?'

He warned, 'It'll be very rough. I'll send you a more accurate one when I've had a chance to crunch the numbers,' and stated an amount a little less than Luke's guess, but not by so much she could feel anything but despair.

She was wondering how on earth she was going to convince a bank manager to lend her enough to cover it when the engineer looked past her and nodded. 'Hello, Luke,' he said. 'Didn't hear you coming.'

Sorrel froze at Luke's deep-voiced answer. Colour abandoned her skin in a chilly tide, but she managed to fix a smile on her lips before she turned.

In the swift glance she allowed herself she noted that he looked grim and a little tired. And the dark, good-looking face was still closed against her.

'Good morning, Sorrel,' he said after he'd greeted the engineer.

Unable to trust her voice, she smiled uncomfortably.

He looked back to the man beside her. 'Job done?'

The engineer glanced from one to the other. 'Yep,' he said. 'I'll send Ms Maitland a proper estimate immediately. How's the new bridge on your place, Luke?'

'Bearing up well,' Luke said drily. 'I'll see you to your car.'

Sorrel held out her hand to the engineer. 'Thanks very much,' she said with another smile, much more open this time.

After they'd shaken hands she went back to Parenga, feeling so cold inside she wondered whether the sun would ever be able to warm her again.

I can't do this, she cried soundlessly to an indifferent universe.

But she gritted her teeth and set her jaw and went up the stairs. She had to cope, even though loving Luke was a life sentence. It was no use wailing to the sun and the moon and the stars for help, because Luke would never trust a beautiful woman. And how could you prove love?

Only by a lifetime of commitment—and that was a choice she'd never be given.

The stepladder she'd found at the back of the garage

was rickety, but it was the only one high enough. Nevertheless she regretted being halfway up it when someone knocked on the door below—a knock followed by Luke's deep voice calling, 'Sorrel!'

She jumped, almost dropping the tray of paint. Beneath her the ladder rocked wildly, then steadied down. 'I'm up here.'

He came silently up the stairs to fill the doorway, frowning when he saw her. 'What the hell are you doing on that wreck of a thing?'

'Painting,' she told him crisply, climbing higher until she could reach the ceiling.

She heard a muttered oath as he strode across the covered carpet and gripped the legs of the ladder.

He said harshly, 'Get off before you fall off.'

'It's all right,' she told him, glancing down to see his eyes narrow, as though he could read every defiant thought surging through her brain. She applied a swathe of white to the ceiling.

'Don't be an idiot. How much painting do you plan to do?'

Sorrel hadn't been conscious of tension knotting her stomach, a knot that intensified when she looked down and saw his lean, strong hands on the ladder only inches from her legs. Stiffly she said, 'The rest of this room and the bathroom next door, to start off with.'

He eyed her with frowning consideration. 'That's a lot of work.'

'So?' she said, applying another swathe of paint.

'So what's giving you circles under your eyes?'

'Paint fumes.' She dipped the roller back in the paint tray, adjusting her weight swiftly as the ladder lurched sideways.

He stilled it and said, 'I'll lend you a decent ladder.'

'How kind of you,' she purred, producing the smile that had lit up thousands of photographs. It was armour, that smile, hiding her thoughts and emotions behind its seductive aloofness. 'But you really don't need to—this ladder might seem rocky, but it's strong. And it's high enough for me to reach the ceiling. I've spent quite a lot of time on it and we understand each other now.'

She was quite proud of her voice; it sounded so normal she decided to push her luck a little further. 'Did you call in for a reason?' she asked, making another sweep across the ceiling.

'To make sure you were all right,' he said shortly.

Absurd to feel a warm glow in the region of her heart. She swallowed. 'I'm fine, thank you. How are you?'

His eyes gleamed as he caught her around the hips and, without breathing any more heavily, lifted her down.

'What the hell—?' she spluttered, clinging to the tray so that no paint landed on the carpet cover.

Luke took the tray and the roller from her hands, dumped them onto a step on the ladder, and as she opened her mouth to protest closed it with a fierce kiss that scrambled her insides and filled her head with the smoke and fumes of desire. Reckless hunger drowned out everything except a mindless clamour for satisfaction.

And then he let her go and stepped back.

Stunned, her heart leaping, Sorrel stared up into eyes that had darkened from threatening grey to dangerous storm clouds. There was nothing soft about the angles and planes of his face, nothing that met or matched the love she'd so reluctantly accepted in herself.

Heart contracting in her breast, she rubbed the back of her hand across her mouth. 'What was that for?'

He watched her as though she was an enemy, his scrutiny as flinty as his voice. 'Punishment, perhaps,' he said, drawling the words with lazy derision.

Sorrel's head came up. Eyes smouldering, she stated, 'There's a word for men who get their kicks hurting women.'

'I know it.' His voice was coldly precise. 'I was punishing myself for being so stupid as to think there might be more to you than a lovely face and a great body.'

Emotion raked her, anger and fear and a humiliating anticipation. 'That,' she said flippantly, 'is all you can expect from a one-night stand.'

'It doesn't have to be a one-night stand.' He spoke with cool control, unyielding eyes in an unyielding face. 'I want you—I've wanted you since you turned eighteen.'

'So you started an affair with Mari O'Neill.' She hid the pain with a scoffing smile.

He said quietly, 'You were just a green kid. I was twenty-five. The last thing you needed was an affair that would end in tears. Mari didn't make the mistake of putting her heart on the line and she was a welcome distraction.'

'How very noble of you,' Sorrel said politely.

He shrugged. 'Nobility didn't come into it—it was self-preservation. Virginal schoolgirls tend to fall pregnant, and their hearts break easily. At that time I couldn't afford to support a child, and I didn't want to hurt you any more than I already had.'

Anger smouldered inside her, but with it a kind of relief that he had wanted her. Ever pragmatic, he'd chosen the simplest way to get them both out of a situation she hadn't been able to deal with.

'But you're not eighteen now,' he said, voice no longer cool. 'And I doubt very much that an affair between us would break your heart. Even if it did, perhaps that would be good for you—you've broken so many in your time.' He startled her by looping his fingers around her wrist, letting his thumb rest over the small throbbing vein there. 'And you still want me, Sorrel.'

She was tempted beyond endurance. More than anything in the world she wanted to forget everything but the fever spinning its rapid heat through her body.

But Luke was offering false coin, counterfeit love, and she didn't dare accept it. He hadn't wanted to kiss her, and when he had she'd sensed resistance as much as passion.

Having an affair with Lucas would be the stupidest thing she could do. He desired the surface glamour of skin and hair and lips and body, whereas she needed so much more.

But most of all, she thought with brittle determination, she needed him out of her system, not embedded even more deeply than he already was.

Get out of here—now! instinct screamed silently, but her brain had seized.

Unconsciously she licked her lips. Luke's eyes narrowed further until all she could see were gleaming splinters of grey, and his hand slid from her wrist to her elbow, turning her and easing her towards him.

With her last shred of will-power Sorrel said, 'No!' and pulled back, jerking free.

'Why not?' he asked, his voice harsh and abrupt.

'Because I don't *do* meaningless affairs,' she said angrily.

'Meaningless?' he said in a neutral voice, but a raw undertone pulled every tiny hair on her skin upright.

She nodded vigorously. 'Meaningless,' she repeated, swallowing because her mouth and throat were suddenly dry. She felt as though she'd stepped up to the edge of a precipice. 'I don't want an affair or a relationship or anything else. Old embers, and all that sort of thing. I'm rather insulted that you think I might be…interested in taking up where we left off just because I'm conveniently right next door. The last thing I need is complications in my life—I want to finish redecorating Parenga.'

She swept a desperate hand around the room, trying to distract herself and him from that dangerous bit of brinkmanship they'd just indulged in.

'Convenient is probably the last word I'd use to describe you,' he said thoughtfully, a blue glint of satirical amusement lighting his eyes.

'I'm not available either,' she told him, trying to sound convincing in spite of her erotic little internal shivers.

One raised brow indicated what he thought of that defiant statement, but he didn't take her up on it.

She met his hooded gaze with her chin angled at him and lips tense, but he'd have to be totally inexperienced not to read the signs her treacherous body was sending out. And he certainly wasn't inexperienced.

'Point taken,' he drawled, the ironic smile hardening his chiselled mouth in savage contrast to his glittering eyes. 'Don't get on that ladder—I'll send someone up with a decent one.' He swung on his heels and left her dazed, the touch of his mouth on hers still tangible. She looked down at her wrist, almost expecting to see his fingerprints on the delicate skin.

'Oh, don't be so bloody stupid!' she snarled, and climbed back up the shaky ladder.

What exactly had he intended?

A raging affair, no strings attached? Which was, presumably, what he had with Mari.

Feverish elation thrummed feverishly through every cell, but beneath it she felt nauseated. 'Damn!' she whispered. 'Damn, damn, damn!'

Baggie uncurled in his patch of sun, pink mouth and white teeth gleaming as he yawned mightily.

'It's all very well for you,' Sorrel said on a half-laugh that sounded suspiciously like a sob. 'You're neutered—sex is no big deal for you! As for love—well, everyone knows that cats are totally self-centred!'

The ladder Luke had promised didn't arrive, which was unlike him. Sorrel, however, had no intention of chasing it up. Painting doggedly, she tried to banish him from her mind by working out where to find the money to fix the bridge.

She'd promised herself this life, this future, and what sort of person would she be if she gave up so easily?

After mulling the possibilities over, she finally made a decision. 'I'll use the money I planned to live on to fix the bridge, and then I'll get a job,' she told the sleeping Baggie. 'I'll contact an agency in Auckland and see if they've got something they can use me for— that would probably be the most lucrative. If they don't want me there are tourists galore around here, so I must be able to find some sort of job that will keep me until I get Parenga up and running.'

A knock on the front door broke into her reverie. 'Coming,' she shouted. The ladder rocked, and she tripped, clutched at air, and fell backwards into pain, and then nothingness.

CHAPTER NINE

'SORREL! Sorrel, can you hear me?'

A man's voice, urgent and filled with concern, was forcing its way past the pounding of her head. Carefully forming the word, she whispered, 'Luke?'

'Yes. Open your eyes for me.'

She winced as she forced her eyelids up. His hard, intent face swam into view, wavering at first. She blinked a couple of times and it steadied. Wonderingly she surveyed tanned skin tautly stretched over a strong foundation, narrowed, piercing eyes and a sinfully beautiful mouth.

'Good,' he said, his deep voice laced with relief. 'Now squeeze my hand.'

Her lashes drifted down. His hand? Oh, he was holding hers. Concentrating, she folded her fingers around his long ones.

'Let it go.' He waited until her hand relaxed. 'Is there any part of you that's really painful?'

She croaked, 'Apart from my head?'

'Yes.'

'My hip,' she muttered. 'My shoulder.'

Quickly and deftly he probed her hip and shoulder. 'I don't think you've broken anything,' he told her when he'd finished. 'You landed on that side so they'll be bruised. Now, I'm going downstairs to get a pillow. Stay still.'

By the time he got back the pounding in her head had decreased a fraction, but the light still hurt her eyes.

Gently Luke lifted her head and slid a pillow under it. 'Did that hurt your neck?'

'No.'

'OK, I'll put a compress on your forehead. Can you hold it there?'

He must have grabbed ice cubes from the fridge and wrapped them in a towel. The icy chill felt wonderful against her aching head. 'Mmm, that's good,' she murmured.

'I'll ring the medical centre.'

He barked into the mobile phone in a way that made Sorrel vaguely sorry for the person on the other end.

'She knocked herself out,' he finished, 'so she should see the doctor... OK, I'll bring her straight in.'

Sorrel lifted her lashes to see him keying in another number. 'Penn, bring the car up to Parenga,' he said without preamble, dark eyes fixed on Sorrel. 'Stack several pillows in it. And a bucket.'

Penn must have said something because he cut her short in a voice so cold it bored through the fog in Sorrel's head, jolting her into awareness. 'Just get here as soon as possible.'

Sorrel closed her eyes against his grim face and said, 'I'm sorry. I don't remember what happened.'

'You fell off that bloody ladder and gave yourself concussion.' His voice came closer. 'Could you get up if I helped you?'

She thought about it for a moment. 'Yes.'

He was wonderfully gentle, and once she was standing he picked her up and carried her down the stairs. Still holding the ice pack against her head, she felt dreamily contented, safe in his arms.

'The car will be here soon,' he told her, the words

rumbling against her, 'and then I'll drive you in to the doctor.'

'I'm being an awful nuisance. Making you sleep on the floor, and then almost drowning myself in the bath, and now this.' She gave a ghostly little laugh. 'I don't suppose you'll believe that until I came back I hadn't had a single accident in ten years?'

'I believe you,' he said. 'How's your head?'

'It's easing off a bit,' Sorrel said, adding, 'You're a good neighbour, Luke.'

'Not good enough,' he said obliquely, shouldering open the front door and setting off down the drive.

Of course she'd forgotten that the bridge was a no-go zone. Eyes clamped shut, she frowned against the bright sunlight. 'I think I can walk now.'

'Not all the way to the road,' he said curtly, 'and not with your eyes closed. Don't worry—you're not very heavy.'

Penn was waiting for them, her face concerned as she opened the back door of the car for Sorrel. 'I've put a couple of pillows in,' she said, 'and the bucket.'

'Thank you,' Sorrel said, trying to smile. 'I won't be sick—I feel much better now.'

Luke eased her gently into the back seat against the pillows, reaching across her to do up her seat belt. 'All right?'

'I'm fine,' she said. But the movement had started her head throbbing again; hastily she closed her eyes and clutched the cold compress to her forehead.

'Do you want me to come in with you?' Penn asked Luke quietly.

'No. She looks like a piece of paper, but she'll be all right. Thank you,' he said, and slid behind the wheel.

The doctor did some poking and prodding in various places of her anatomy, shone a light into her eyes, prescribed a cream for the bruises, and sent her on her way with instructions to rest for twenty-four hours under observation.

'No driving and no sport, of course,' he said to Luke outside the surgery, after detailing a list of symptoms to watch for during that time. He smiled at Sorrel. 'But she looks a pretty tough character to me. Just keep an eye on her.'

In the car Sorrel said with some of her usual crispness, 'Thank you for everything you've done, but you don't need to worry. I feel almost human again.'

'If you're trying to tell me that you don't want to come home to Waimanu with me, forget it,' Luke ordered, backing skilfully out of the car park. 'Why didn't you use the ladder I sent up?'

'What ladder?'

'Sorrel—'

Her spurt of energy evaporating, she leaned back against the pillows as he set the car in motion. Wearily she told him, 'If you'd sent up a ladder I'd have used it.'

The dark, tangible force of his anger surged through the car, but he didn't say anything more than, 'Anyway, you've only got one bed at Parenga.'

'So?' Her astonishment made two syllables of the word.

'You heard the doctor—you should be under observation for twenty-four hours. If I stay the night at Parenga I'll have to share your bed, because I am not sleeping on the floor or in one of those chairs.'

Beneath the teasing note in his voice she heard determination. 'Oh, all right. I'm not feeling strong enough to fight with you,' she yielded on a sigh. 'Waimanu it'll be.'

'Now I am alarmed,' he said. 'Such meek acquiescence!'

She could tell that he was smiling. Her heart twisted, but she retorted, 'Enjoy it while it lasts.'

At Waimanu she refused to let him carry her, saying stubbornly, 'I can walk. The headache's easing off now, and my legs work fine.'

'It didn't last long,' Luke said, deadpan. He watched her take a couple of tentative steps. 'You're still a bit shaky.'

His arm around her shoulders supported her up the stairs and into the spare bedroom, with Penn in close attendance. Sorrel told herself sternly that this care and concern wasn't personal—a man who protected ducklings on his lawn would do his best for anyone who'd been hurt.

'I brought along some of your clothes and toiletries from Parenga,' the housekeeper said. 'I hope you don't mind me going through your things…'

Perched on the side of the bed, Sorrel gave a resigned smile. 'Of course not. Anyway, I bet Luke told you to.'

'I did,' Luke said calmly. 'Penn will stay until you're in bed. If you need anything, ring the bell.' He indicated the bedside table, where a small bronze bell waited. 'I'll go to Parenga and clear up the mess the paint made when you dropped the tray.'

The housekeeper said quickly, 'That's been done.'

'Good.' Dark eyes cool and objective, Luke examined Sorrel closely, then, apparently satisfied, said, 'If you feel up to it later you can come down for dinner.'

Sorrel watched him walk out of the room before turning to the housekeeper, who asked hastily, 'Do you want a shower?'

'I'd love one, but, whatever Luke says, I really don't need you in attendance. Apart from the remains of the headache and a few aches and pains I feel pretty good, and you must have other things to do.'

Penn gave her a constrained smile. 'Around here we're used to doing what the man says. I'll wait until you're in bed.'

Later, dressed in a loose, comfortable T-shirt and a pair of knickers, Sorrel lay in bed and sighed.

The headache had retreated to a dull, barely noticeable throb, but it didn't seem a good idea to read or watch television. Although Penn had delivered a large jug of delicious lime juice and some tempting little cakes, Sorrel wasn't hungry and there was only so much liquid she could drink.

She tried very hard to nap, but every cell in her body was alert, excited by the nearness of the man she loved. Useless to tell herself that this was merely a truce; her foolish heart was a fifth columnist, working at her downfall from within.

She watched clouds creep by in a blue, blue sky; without a sea breeze the air was so still that more clouds built over the land, and by dusk thunder was rumbling gently around the hills.

A slight tap at the door brought her upright in the bed. Head swimming slightly, she called, 'Come in.'

It was Luke, filling the room with his powerful presence. 'How do you feel?'

Men with his unforced, prowling sexuality—a sexuality backed by his innate authority and total competence—ought to be locked up. They did too much damage to impressionable feminine hearts.

'Bored,' Sorrel told him frankly, fighting back a singing joy.

His keen steel-grey gaze lanced across her face. 'Do you want dinner up here or downstairs?'

'Downstairs,' she declared with fervour. 'I love this room, but I already know it too well.'

His smile showed strong white teeth. 'How's your head?'

'The headache's almost gone.'

'I'll wait outside until you're ready.'

Penn had brought down elegantly tailored trousers, left over from Sorrel's modelling days, and a silk shirt in a clear soft honey-yellow that turned her eyes into golden jewels. After combing her hair cautiously, to avoid the bump on the back of her head, she emerged.

Luke turned away from the large abstract oil painting hung in the hall and checked her over again. 'All right?'

'Fine,' she told him. 'The bump is developing nicely, but it doesn't hurt unless I touch it. I'm a fraud.'

He didn't answer that, merely offered his arm. Chilled, Sorrel rested her fingertips on it and let herself be escorted down.

Penn served them a superb meal; it was a pity Sorrel's appetite had disappeared with Luke's arrival. However, with a mixture of persuasion and gentle bullying he saw to it that she ate more than she'd thought she wanted.

And while he was doing this he led the conversation smoothly, so that before long she found herself indulging in an animated and absorbing discussion of a book they'd both recently read.

'Would you like something to drink?' he asked later.

'Alcohol isn't appropriate, but I'm sure Penn can find something more interesting than that water for you.'

'Water's perfectly all right; if you want wine feel free to have it.' She ate an asparagus tip, delicate and succulent, silkily enrobed in butter.

'Water's fine for me too,' he said, and glanced at her plate. 'Ten years ago you had a much better appetite.'

His words hung on the air, deliberate and flat.

Sorrel kept her gaze down for several seconds. 'Ten years ago I hadn't finished growing up.'

'You mean you hadn't yet learned to starve yourself.'

'Normally I eat very well,' she said. 'Don't believe everything you read about starving models. Only women with our particular set of genetic traits make it in the business. Sure, some go to dangerous lengths to diet, but most eat normally.'

'So your lack of appetite tonight is a result of your fall?'

She put down her knife and fork. 'Probably,' she evaded.

Luke leaned back in his chair, long fingers loosely clasping his water glass, his eyes uncompromising and hard as they scanned her face. 'No sign of nausea?' he asked. 'No double vision?'

'None whatsoever. I got off lightly.' She set her jaw and ploughed on with the apology she'd been rehearsing since she arrived at Waimanu. 'I'm sorry I used that wretched ladder. I seem to have done nothing but stupid things ever since I came back, and unfortunately you've had to pick up the pieces. When you said that my life might impinge on yours, I scoffed, but you were right. From now on I'll be more careful.'

'If it's time for apologies, I've got one too. I told someone to take a decent ladder up to you, but didn't think to check that it had arrived.' His tone and eyes as hard as quartz promised retribution for whoever had been negligent.

'Luke, that's not your fault,' she said, shocked that he should think so. Of course it was typical of the man; over the years so many people had depended on him that he automatically assumed responsibility.

'If I'd made sure it got there, you wouldn't have fallen.'

'It wasn't your fault,' she repeated. 'Please don't think that—I'd hate to feel that what I've been thinking is nice New Zealand neighbourliness is just guilt. I don't associate you with guilt!'

Luke laughed, and for a moment a fragile camaraderie warmed her. 'Oh, I've done things I'm guilty about,' he said drily. 'Anyway, your ladder is now reposing in a heap of splinters on the bonfire.'

Sorrel's mouth opened. She met gleaming grey eyes, and said with rigid courtesy, 'I'm so grateful you saved me from having to carry it there myself.'

He grinned. 'It was nothing. See if you can eat some more of that chicken before Penn brings in pudding.'

It was more of a command than a suggestion, but delivered in a voice like a caress. Flushing, she applied herself to another couple of mouthfuls, and by the time she'd finished she'd regained her composure.

She did refuse the delicious dessert Penn brought in, and coffee afterwards. The apologies had cleared the air, and, while she was still very aware of the effect Luke's intense masculinity had on her, she felt that they'd achieved a more durable truce. It was probably her brittle state too; Luke treated her with an exquisite courtesy tinged with subtle, low-key flirtation. Relaxing, she dropped her guard enough to talk on until she startled herself with a huge yawn.

'Bed,' Luke said abruptly, and got up.

Sorrel followed suit, only to find the room swirling around her. She grabbed the edge of the table and closed her eyes.

'Sorrel!'

He came around the table in a silent lunge, pulling her against his chest, arms catching her around the waist and holding her upright.

'It's all right—I just stood up too fast.' Cautiously she opened her eyes, relieved when the room stopped dipping and swaying.

Luke said, 'Are you sure?'

It was too easy to lie against him and accept the support he offered. Straightening her backbone, she said firmly, 'Certain.'

True, her breasts were heavy and tender under the silk shirt, her body warm and lax and intensely responsive, but such an alarming sensitivity had nothing to do with her head.

He turned her in his arms, measured her with narrowed, perceptive eyes, and startled her by picking her up and carrying her across to the door.

'This is getting to be a habit,' she said in a tight, small voice, all of that lovely ease and relaxation fled. Held so close to him, she flinched as the heat of his body enfolded her and stripped the strength from her bones.

'You don't look capable of walking,' he told her roughly.

'Of course I can…' Her breathless words so shocked her she bit off the rest of the sentence.

He said nothing, but his arms tightened as he nego-tiated the doorway into the hall.

Sorrel drew a ragged breath into painfully com-pressed lungs and gazed stiffly ahead until slowly, with excruciating care, he lowered her onto the bed. She looked up, and sizzled in hot blue flames.

He's going to kiss me, she thought, half-horrified, half-exultant, as she closed her eyes and fought a bitter battle with herself.

And I'm going to kiss him back...

Resist it though she might, she wanted the touch of Luke's mouth rather more than she wanted to breathe.

And she couldn't deny him, just as she'd never been able to deny him before. The dark enchantment of the senses still held. Only Luke, she thought. Only ever Luke...

'I'll take off your shoes,' he said, and crouched to unbuckle her sandals.

She nodded, watching the pulse in his tanned throat. When he slid the leather strap free his cool hands brushed her ankle, sending electricity stabbing through her. She was fascinated by the blue sparks in his eyes—compelling, almost hypnotic against the grey iris. Elec-tricity coalesced into heat and fire in the pit of her stom-ach.

He leaned forward a little and began to massage her feet, running his thumbs over the fine bones of her ankles and the high arches.

His touch, and the sight of his black head so close to her, summoned a wild, painful expectancy.

'There you are,' he said and looked up to catch her watching him. He froze, and then he touched her cheek, and her mouth, slowly, almost tenderly. The fiery blue lights in his eyes danced recklessly. 'Sorrel, tell me to stop.'

Above the soft murmur of the river his voice was thick and uneven. Sorrel fell into the molten depths of his eyes; she leaned forward and groaned softly as his mouth met hers.

This kiss was different—more tender, deeper, more gentle than any other. When it was over she found herself lying against him on the bed, listening to the rapid sound of his heart with a bemused smile.

And then he said in a low, self-derisory voice, 'I'm certain this isn't what the doctor meant when he said to keep you under observation.'

'No,' she said dazedly, aware of a dull thud behind her eye.

He eased her back onto the pillow. 'I'm sorry,' he said abruptly. 'I didn't intend that to happen. How's your head?'

'Letting me know it's there,' she sighed.

He said something under his breath while he stroked her cheek and forehead in slow sweeps. 'You're exhausted, and no wonder. I'll go now—try to get a good night's sleep. I'll come in during the night just to make sure you're all right, so don't be scared if you hear me moving around. Goodnight, Sorrel.'

'Goodnight, Luke.' She bit her lip because the words sounded bereft. 'And thank you for everything.'

Sleep refused to submerge her in the oblivion she craved. For a long time she stared out at the silent glory of the stars and listened to the river sweep by. Luke came in several times and stood beside the bed in silence, and each time she pretended to sleep, until eventually she did.

*   *   *

Over the dinner table the next evening Sorrel announced that she was going home the following day.

'All right,' Luke said, as though he had the right to grant permission, 'but I'll come up a couple of times a day to see how you're getting on.'

He'd worked out his tactics the preceding night, when he'd stood by her bed listening to her breathe. She could have hurt herself much more severely. Even now he felt sick at the memory of her graceful body crumpled on the floor.

Sorrel eyed him with irritation. 'My head's fine,' she said spiritedly.

'What about the bruises?' Although her face wasn't the paper-white that had shocked him so much yesterday she still looked delicate.

She pulled a face. 'They're going to be dramatic, but the cream helps.'

'Don't do any more painting or sanding—anything that requires effort on your part.'

When she didn't answer he said with silky menace, 'Sorrel?'

'You have no right to set conditions,' she returned, her lush mouth obstinate.

His smile was lethal. 'If you don't promise me that you won't do anything more than a little gentle housework I'll tie you to that bed upstairs.' It wasn't like him to make wild threats, but he'd do whatever it took to stop her doing anything that might put her recovery back.

She measured glances with him. 'I know you mean well, but—' she began.

'It probably took ten years off my life to see you on the floor. If I'd made sure the ladder had got up to Parenga, it wouldn't have happened.'

Yes, that was the way to play it. The smouldering brilliance of her big eyes was transformed into instant comprehension, and her mouth gentled. He remembered the feel of it beneath his and his body hardened unbearably.

'Luke, please don't blame yourself,' she said swiftly.

He shrugged. 'I do. Penn will prepare your dinner each night until the doctor clears you.'

Ignoring her half-eaten meal, she leaned forward and glared at him. 'Do you ever give up?'

'No,' he said calmly.

Temper lent a glow to her exquisite ivory skin and a glitter in the gold-green eyes. Heat and hunger hit him like the fierce blast from a bushfire. His fingers curled on his knife. It took him a second to relax them enough to let it drop onto the tablecloth.

She clearly wasn't up to par, because she satisfied herself with another mutinous look before saying levelly, 'I hadn't planned to do any work until the doctor said it was all right.'

The following morning she sat beside him in the car and thanked him, sounding absurdly stilted. 'I didn't have to climb that wretched ladder, you know,' she finished.

Luke gave a slanting smile that released a slow flood of sweet fire through her. 'Just take care from now on.'

So she did.

He came up two or three times each day, careful not to touch her or do anything that might lead to another kiss. Sorrel knew that this cool detachment was sensible, but as the bruises faded it grew more difficult to cope with the need that gnawed her every time she saw him—or even thought of him.

'I can't come tomorrow,' he said one afternoon as

they met on the road, he in his car, she striding towards the beach with Baggie.

Sorrel resented the disappointment that ached through her. 'That's all right,' she said airily, smiling at him with a determination that made her cheeks ache. 'You really don't need to be so religious about checking on me—I'm fine now.'

He got out of the car, overpowering and lethal and more than a little predatory. 'I've got a round of meetings in Whangarei, and at least one of them will run late. I might have to stay there.'

'Have fun,' she said flippantly, and, to show him that she didn't really care whether he came to see her or not, she raised her hand and casually patted his cheek. His hand came up to hold hers there, and he turned his face into the palm and kissed it, his lips lingering with erotic intensity against her skin.

Sharp, delicious needles of sensation pierced her.

'Then again,' he said softly against her mouth, 'I might not.'

He released her and she stepped back, pink-cheeked and breathless.

That kiss stayed with her all night and into the next day, a teasing, tormenting promise.

At lunchtime she put down her paintbrush and went down to make a sandwich. She'd just finished eating it when she heard a knock at the front door. Frowning slightly, she went to open it.

Small, blonde and voluptuous, the woman who waited for her said, 'Hello, Sorrel. It's been a long time.'

'Mari.' Sorrel swallowed. 'Come in.'

'Thanks.' Mari O'Neill looked around with composure. 'I see you're redecorating.'

At a disadvantage in her paint-spotted T-shirt and elderly shorts, Sorrel said, 'Yes. Would you like a cup of coffee? Some lunch?'

The other woman gave a wry smile. 'No, thanks. I need to talk to you.'

Her shock expanding into an icy void, Sorrel led the way into the room Cynthia had always called the small parlour. The two chairs and a table looked out over a brick patio scented with gardenias and roses, her god-mother's favourite flowers.

They sat down. Mari examined her expensive Italian shoes and said, 'Did you know that Luke and I have been lovers for years?'

CHAPTER TEN

NOT trusting herself to speak, Sorrel nodded.

'I assumed that eventually we'd get married,' Mari said quietly. 'Oh, it was never spoken of; we are—were—good friends, and Luke made it quite clear that he was happy with the status quo. And most of the time I was happy too—I've got a demanding job, and, well…' she made an aimless gesture before letting her hands drop back into her lap '…it worked.'

'I don't think—'

'Bear with me, please.'

But Mari paused so long before she began again that Sorrel gave her an anxious look. She saw nothing beyond a skilfully made-up face, calm and serene.

Mari said slowly, 'The thing is, of course, I fell in love with him. It's very easy to do.' Her smile was tinged with wry sympathy when she looked across at Sorrel. 'As you found out. Apart from being magnificent in bed, he's got a brilliant brain and he really listens to what you have to say—so many men don't.'

Sorrel bit her lip.

'But he didn't fall in love with me,' the clear, remorseless voice went on. 'Because of his bitch of a mother and that appalling stepmother I don't think he'll ever trust a woman enough to love her. When he marries—and he will, because he's a Hardcastle and he wants a son to inherit Waimanu—he'll choose a wife with just as much care and just as cold-bloodedly as he breeds his pedigree stock.' She looked up at Sorrel, her

163

eyes magnified by tears. 'It's not going to be me, and it won't be you, either. You're everything he distrusts—beautiful, sophisticated, sexually active.'

Sorrel made a small, shocked sound.

Mari shrugged. 'He's not a hypocrite, but he dislikes promiscuity. So he despises himself because he's never been able to get you out of his system. Of course it didn't help to have your face splashed over massive billboards and in every magazine and newspaper for years.'

'How do you know all this?' Sorrel's voice was low and tightly controlled. She had no intention of refuting Mari's hint at her supposed promiscuity; two men, she thought fiercely, did not make for a wildly abandoned love life, but the gossip columnists tarred all models with the same brush.

'I know him very well,' Mari said, her mouth tightening. 'I liked you all those years ago, and that's why I've come. To warn you. He'll be a magnificent lover, but don't let him keep you dangling like he did me. Believe me—' her voice broke but she caught herself up and finished evenly '—the game isn't worth the candle.'

She got to her feet with a pale smile. 'At least you've acted as a catalyst,' she said without emotion. 'I might have gone on wasting my time if you hadn't come back. Remember once I told you that the woman always chooses—and you said that Luke would do his own choosing? I wish I'd listened to you. Goodbye—and good luck.'

Sorrel watched her walk down the drive and over the bridge, listened to the sound of her car until it faded away.

Mute agony scythed through her, holding her pris-

ROBYN DONALD

165

oner until she forced herself back to work. Mari's words had only reinforced a truth she'd refused to face: Luke's distrust of women went so deep that he'd probably never be able to overcome it.

What was she going to do? Accept him as he was, or pull up the drawbridge and refuse him?

Each choice offered unending pain. She realised she'd been staring at the wall without doing anything for some minutes, her brain desperately seeking ways out of the impasse. Moving slowly, she climbed down from the ladder, automatically tipping paint back into the can before washing the roller.

'Come on, Baggie,' she said in a voice flat with repressed despair, 'let's go for a walk on the beach.'

She walked too long beneath the blazing sun before seeking refuge under the sheltering limbs of a pohutukawa. Thoughts tossing endlessly around her tired brain, she stared blindly out across the glittering sea, deaf to the whisper of waves on the white-hot sand and the ugly screams of a pack of gulls fighting over something on the tideline.

I'm not going to run away, she thought, picking up a handful of sand, mercifully cool in the deep shade of the tree, and letting it sift through her fingers. I have to stick this out.

So either she became Luke's new mistress, to be abandoned in her turn when he found a suitable candidate for his planned, bloodless marriage, or she cut off all communication between them except the most impersonal.

She looped her arms around her knees and rested her head on them, listening to the uneven beat of her heart. Pride chose the latter course, but what if loving him without conditions, without hope and without limit could restore his lost trust?

Stupid, she scoffed. Rescued by the love of a good woman? It hadn't worked for Mari, and it wouldn't work for her.

One night at Parenga might have taught her that she loved Luke, but she wasn't going to sacrifice years of her life in a useless, heartbreaking attempt to persuade him that she was loyal and trustworthy.

'Like a dog,' she said bitterly, scrambling up and brushing the sand off her legs. 'Time to go home, Baggie.'

Tomorrow she'd ring a contact in Auckland, seeking work; it would keep her away from the house, but surely if she made Parenga her base that would fulfil the conditions in Cynthia's will. Then she'd sell, and make a new life somewhere else.

Her hand stole up to clench over her heart, as though she could stop its bleak anguish with sheer will-power. In time she'd get over Luke, because this time she'd decided to leave.

Tonight, when he came back, she'd tell him she didn't want to take their relationship—if you could call it that—any further. Unless she was misreading that final kiss that morning...

No. There had been too much significance in his smile, in that fleeting caress. He wanted her, and he meant to have her, presumably to get her out of his system.

She was staring at her uneaten dinner when the telephone went—Luke on his mobile.

'Hi,' she said, her heart jittering crazily in her breast. 'How did your day go?'

'Good,' he said. 'I should be at Parenga in half an hour.'

'I—OK. Fine. See you then.'

It was an oddly formal conversation—no, she thought bleakly, not formal. Impersonal.

Perhaps she hadn't had to make that painful choice on the beach. Perhaps he'd already made it for her.

A mixture of shock and agitation drove her into the garden. Baggie prowling at her heels, she paced through the scented evening until she saw a movement down by the bridge.

Trembling, she stopped under the magnolia tree and rested her hand on its cool bark. The setting sun, a golden ball in a dramatic scarlet sky, caught Luke's black head, turning it into sable fire. He'd left his car down by the road and was walking across the bridge with a confidence that bordered on arrogance.

Baggie strolled down to meet him; two imperious males, Sorrel thought, trying to banish the chill seeping through her.

She'd changed out of her paint-spotted jeans into long sleek trousers, and topped them with a loose smock the same pale gold as her eyes, tying her hair up onto the top of her head in a ponytail. Clothes seemed very fragile armour, but they were all she had.

'You look intriguingly artistic,' Luke observed as he came up the drive, hard grey eyes surveying her with an assessing glint.

She gave him her most remote smile. 'And you look for all the world like a tycoon. How did your meetings go?'

He wore tailored trousers that reinforced the power of his long legs, and a shirt subtly cut to reveal the blatant width of his shoulders. Sexual confidence and energy radiated from him in a sensual aura that targeted her every nerve.

'Well enough,' he said. 'Ask me in.'

Sorrel observed him through her lashes. He looked tired and grim, his expression set in lines of controlled detachment. Pain squeezed her heart. 'Is there something powerfully symbolic about inviting you into Parenga?'

'Stop fencing with me, Sorrel. I need to talk to you.'

'All right,' she said stiffly, almost flinching at his final words, exactly the same as Mari's. 'Come in.'

Once in the parlour, she didn't offer him a drink. She did sit down, but he stood at the window looking out over the garden.

Tension spiked through the room, tightening her skin in the age-old response to danger. When she couldn't bear it any longer she asked abruptly, 'What's happened?'

'For starters,' he said with forbidding detachment, turning to face her so that all she could see of him was his outline against the crimson sky outside, 'what did Mari say to you this afternoon?'

Shock held her speechless.

'Mari has apparently made a confidante of Penn.' His voice gave nothing away. 'Penn told her when your box arrived, and when Mari left here today she went down to Waimanu to see Penn. Who rang me when she'd left.'

'So that's why—?'

'Yes, that's why Penn's been distant. It's also why she didn't pass on my message about the ladder. I told her to tell one of the farmhands to bring it up. She didn't.' His face hardened into ruthless lines. 'For

which she's very sorry—and not just because she almost lost her job. She didn't intend any harm to you.'

'I'm sure she didn't.'

He said remotely, 'It won't happen again.' He looked
around the room as though he'd never seen it before.
'What did Mari say?'

'Nothing I didn't already know,' Sorrel returned with
spirit.

Luke's half-closed eyes gleamed. 'Tell me,' he said
in a gentle tone that sent shudders scudding the length
of her spine.

'Are you still seeing her?'

His head came up. She could read nothing in his
expression, nothing in his voice when he said, 'No,'
but the soft, deadly syllable shook her as shouting and
fury would never have.

Nevertheless she said levelly, 'And you're not seeing
me, so you have no right to hear details of a conversation between two people who mean nothing to you.'

He stared at her, eyes molten, mouth compressed into
a white line. 'What the hell do you mean—I'm not
seeing you?'

Sorrel took a deep, painful breath and forced the
words past a painful constriction in her throat. 'If you
want the same arrangement that you had with Mari, I'm
afraid I'm not good mistress material.'

He pinned her with a cruelly speculative scrutiny that
brought stinging colour to her skin. 'Oh, I'm sure
you're just being modest,' he drawled silkily, coming
towards her with purposeful strides.

She braced herself. She couldn't bear it if he kissed
her in anger, in lust and contempt.

Of course he saw it; he stopped a stride away, his

face grim. 'What's the matter? You know I won't hurt you.'

'Luke, please don't do this.' She dragged in a shivering breath and he closed his eyes a second before transfixing her with a glittering gaze.

His voice cold and unsparing, he asked, 'Tell me, how do you plan to pay for the bridge?'

'I'll manage,' she said remotely.

'No doubt. Would it make things simpler if I offered you a loan—on very easy terms, of course?' He looked at her with a disturbing mixture of anger and desire. 'Perhaps with enough extra so that you can afford to hire renovators for the house? What price do you put on yourself?'

Without volition her hand swung at his face. He didn't move, not even when the imprint of her fingers was branded red on his cheek.

Her hot colour drained away, leaving her pale and cold. 'I am not a prostitute,' she whispered, sick with humiliated anger.

'You're certainly no shrinking, virginal violet.' He surveyed her as though she disgusted him, as though disgusted with himself for wanting her. 'Perhaps I've been too blunt. Let's call it security I'm offering. It means the same thing but it sounds better. The sex was fantastic—how much do you think it would be worth on a regular basis?'

'Nothing without love,' she said angrily.

He laughed.

How many times had she read about breaking hearts and thought it a tired, worn-out cliché? But she felt hers shatter, split from top to bottom to splinter into fragments, each one a sliver of agony. It hurt so much she could only survive by summoning anger to temporarily ease the pain of grief.

'So you're just like all the others,' she said savagely.

'Others?' he asked. And when she shook her head and turned her face away, he demanded, 'What others are you talking about?'

'There are plenty of men out there like you, Luke, prepared to pay for the kudos of having a minor celebrity share their bed. Is that what you want?' she asked, goading him because if she didn't she'd shame herself by breaking down and howling. 'A mistress just along the road? Fantastic sex whenever you decide to take it?'

He was right—love entailed disillusion and pain; she should have settled for casual sex. It would have been so much easier to live for the moment and keep her heart locked away from pain. If she'd done that she wouldn't be longing for anything other than what Luke could give—honest commerce.

He said nothing, just held her with a narrowed stare that summoned stinging colour up through her skin. High in the maple tree outside a tui sang his evening aria, his heart throbbing through the glorious song. A soft breeze billowed the curtains inward, bringing a gust of gardenia-scented air.

Finally Luke said, 'I want you.'

Stark, simple and true; she couldn't doubt his honesty. Or his determination; it smouldered in his eyes, roughened his voice, radiated from him. So Mari had been right.

In spite of everything his words fanned passionate desire deep inside Sorrel, summoned flames and a scorching sexuality. But his admission wasn't enough.

She knew she didn't have the stamina to love him and receive only lust in return.

Unable to think, almost unaware of what she was saying, she demanded in a raw voice, 'Is this the arrangement you had with Mari? Sex in return for money?'

'No.' He looked down at her with a closed, hard face. 'I was going to marry Mari.'

Sorrel flung out a hand to grasp the back of the nearest chair, clinging to it with white knuckles until she could draw a breath that didn't stab her. With dilated eyes she searched Luke's dark, unyielding face. 'Why didn't you?'

'Because you sent a box to Parenga,' he told her evenly. 'And I discovered that I'd been marking time, waiting for you to come back. Once I realised that, I also realised I couldn't marry another woman with you still lodged under my skin.'

Oh, Mari did know him very well. Sorrel said thinly, 'Why do you hate me so much?'

His head came up. 'I don't hate you,' he said curtly.

'You think I'm like your stepmother.'

'No. She would never have given up a high-flying career to care for a man like your father, paralysed and unable to talk.' He paused, dark eyes surveying her face, then went on deliberately, 'Especially not if he'd lost every cent she earned playing roulette and backing horses.'

Sorrel's jaw dropped. For a moment she couldn't breathe, but she rallied to ask in a shaken voice, 'How did you find out?'

'It's easy enough if you know where to look,' he said dismissively. 'When you dropped so dramatically out of sight there were rumours—of marriage, drug addiction, bankruptcy. Cynthia confided once that your father was a gambler—it worried her. So when I realised you had no money I made enquiries. The results came through last night.'

Sorrel turned abruptly away. 'You had no right to pry,' she said, pronouncing each word carefully.

Luke's merciless voice went on, 'You wouldn't have told me.' It wasn't a question.

'Of course not.' She looked down at hands twisting together in the classical gesture of helplessness. Stopping them, forcing them to hang limply at her sides, gave her something to concentrate on. 'Why should I? You wouldn't have believed me. And if you had,' she said with a spurt of malice, 'you'd have assumed that I'd come back to seduce money from you.'

'Why didn't you take on another perfume campaign?' he asked with silky contempt. 'I can vouch that your body is still as beautiful and provocative as it was when you did the last one.'

The skin on the back of her neck prickled. Stiffening her shoulders, she said dully, 'I—needed the money.'

'I hope they paid you well. It certainly caused controversy, so I suppose it did what it was supposed to do.' He didn't have to say what he thought about the campaign. The edge of contempt in his tone said it for him.

'Luke,' she said, shaken and exhausted but still valiant, 'please go. This isn't getting us anywhere, and I'm tired.'

After a silent tense moment, he swivelled on his heel and left without a word.

Sorrel waited until the front door closed before collapsing into a chair and beginning to weep—painful, difficult tears that wrenched through her and brought her no relief.

Eventually she got up and went to wash her face, knowing now that staying at Parenga was out of the question.

She was dragging her way to bed when the knocker on the front door sounded in several sharp, staccato knocks. 'No,' she whispered. 'Oh, please no.'

It didn't stop, so she opened the door.

'You'd better get a peephole put into this,' Luke said curtly, walking in.

He sounded normal, but she sensed a dark rage in him that had her falling back.

Leading the way into the bookroom she enquired dully, 'What do you want?'

'You asked me that before. I want you.' In a voice rigid with some strong emotion he said, 'I've spent the past ten years waiting for you to come back. I didn't furnish the other rooms at Waimanu because I wanted you to do them. I don't know anything about love, but I know about wanting.' He stopped, big hands clenching at his sides. Then he added starkly, 'And needing.'

Afraid to move, to speak, she stared at him with huge, dilating eyes.

He said, 'Sorrel, have I spoiled everything so much that it's beyond repair? Can you forgive me? I've been mad since you came back, fighting this…this desperation. I thought making love to you might sate it, but although it was a miracle it simply made me want you more.'

'It's not enough,' she said heavily. 'I couldn't live with distrust. And you don't trust me.'

'I want to care for you, protect you from anything that might hurt you or worry you or upset you.' He spoke dispassionately, his tone at odds with the words. When she stayed silent he finished, 'I want to come home at night and know you're there for me. I want you to bear my children. You mean more to me than anyone I've ever known. Surely that indicates some degree of trust?'

She should have been ecstatic.

Yet it wasn't enough.

'I've heard a lot about what *you* want,' she said. 'You've never asked me what I want.'

She read anger in his eyes, and a coldness that shook her, and then he turned away with a swift, slicing gesture. Harshly, as though each word was painful, he said, 'So tell me.'

'I want you,' she said simply, knowing she couldn't go back now, gambling with her life and his for higher stakes. 'Because I love you, Luke. I can't remember a time when I didn't. But I'm not going to be a partner in an uneven relationship—as your father was.'

Luke went white. He stared at her for several seconds before swinging on his heel and striding across to the window. Cynthia's roses glimmered in the darkness, and from beyond came the hush of the sea—eternal, sad, inexorable.

He said uncompromisingly, 'Love made him into a weak, whimpering fool, and I vowed I'd have nothing to do with it.'

Sorrel's mouth dried. She heard her heart beating wildly as she waited.

He turned his head and looked at her, eyes hooded and hard. 'But it seems I don't get a choice. Love isn't something you can organise or control; it chooses its own way, and its own time.'

'I think we do get a choice,' she said, speaking

slowly because this was hugely important to both of them. 'Sex—no. That's physical. But love—I love you because as well as being the most exciting man I've ever met you're honourable and hard-working and kind and intelligent and I—you're a man I respect.' Tears ached at the back of her eyes as she chanced everything on this final throw. 'But respect must be a two-way thing.'

'I admire you more than I can ever tell you,' he said quietly. 'You looked after your father when he'd betrayed you, you came here ready to work on Parenga, you're bright and gentle and nobody's fool, you were prepared to risk your life to save a blasted con artist of a cat—and you're so beautiful you stop my heart.'

'I won't always be beautiful,' she said, a tiny frown pleating her brow. She shot a fleeting glance his way, but could make out nothing in his face; his formidable self-control rebuffed all attempts to discover his real feelings.

'You will always be beautiful to me,' he said with such simple conviction that she at last had the proof she needed so badly. 'The moment I saw you again I knew I was in trouble. And when I found you unconscious I had to accept that something had taken me over, and I couldn't control either it or myself.'

He looked at her with something very like bitterness. He still hadn't admitted that he loved her, but this was what she'd longed for without realising it until she came back—Luke's trust, freely offered, willingly given.

Shaking, she repeated his words as though making a vow. 'Luke, I want to care for you, protect you from anything that might hurt you or worry you or upset you. I want to come home at night and know you're there

for me. I want you to be the father of my children. And
I will love you all my life.'

He covered the floor separating them in two long
strides and caught her up against him, holding her so
close she couldn't breathe.

When she began to struggle he loosed her; she lifted
her face to meet his, and they kissed.

This time their loving was long and sweet and
tender—so tender that when it was over and she was
lying in his arms, her head on his shoulder, her hand
smoothing over the sleek, taut skin of his hip, Sorrel
was certain that nothing in her life could ever match
this.

'Why did Mari come here?' he asked, stroking the
damp fall of chestnut hair back from her cheek.

The other woman's name intruded into her cocoon
of joy. 'To warn me that you'd be perfectly happy with
a relationship provided I didn't want anything more
than sex and companionship.'

He called Mari something that made Sorrel wince.
'After you left Parenga we became lovers for six
months or so,' he said flatly. 'We only got back together again about a year ago; I liked her, I respected
her, and so I decided she'd make a good wife. I knew
she wouldn't refuse me, because she's level-headed and
sensible. Then you sent that box back and all my cold-
blooded, pragmatic plans crashed in disarray around
me. I think I must have been crazy with—oh, fear, I
suppose.'

'Fear?'

He said harshly, 'The night my stepmother came into
my bedroom clad in a nightgown and nothing else I
promised myself that I'd never be like my father, never
let a woman get under my skin so that I lost not only

autonomy, but every scrap of integrity.' His arms tightened around him and in his voice she could hear the
echoes of that long ago betrayal. 'He loved me, but
although he knew what Cherie was—that she'd bleed
Waimanu of every cent—it didn't stop him from doing
his best to disinherit me.'

'You're not like that,' she said fiercely.

'Perhaps not, but when your box arrived I thought,
She's coming back! And my life suddenly turned from
workaday grey to a rainbow of colours. That was when
I realised I was too much like him to be safe.' He kissed
the satiny skin of her throat. 'Yet I couldn't marry
Mari, so I broke it off with her as gently as I could. I
don't blame her for wanting revenge.'

Sorrel recalled the woman's face and knew that Mari
loved him and had fought for him in the only way she
knew how. Wisely, she said nothing.

Sombrely Luke went on, 'I'm not proud of myself
for hurting her, and even less proud of blaming you for
my own weakness and behaving like an arrogant bas-
tard when you arrived back.'

Showing her teeth in something a little less friendly
than a smile, Sorrel pushed herself up and examined
his angular face, so beloved, so uncompromising.

'Why did you?' she asked. 'I can understand why
you were afraid to love—your father's problems would
have put anyone off!' She poked a long forefinger into
his chest. 'But you *knew* me—I'd more or less shad-
owed you for years, and we'd always got on quite well.
You'd been a kind, aloof big-brother figure for years,
yet you acted as though my modelling course had come
with a character transplant!'

Luke looked at her with narrowed, burning eyes and
said with brutal self-contempt, 'I'd just got rid of

Cherie, who'd done her best to destroy my father and me, and then you arrived—beautiful, forbidden and a powerful threat to my self-image. About a nano-second after I saw you I realised that somehow, over those big-brother years, you'd stolen away an essential part of me. I started manufacturing anger and resentment to hide a terrified self-disgust.'

'You? I don't believe it!' She stared at him, read the truth of his statement in his eyes, and her heart sang, because he was no longer hiding himself behind the handsome mask of his face.

'Believe it,' he said briefly, and pulled her down to lie on top of him. 'I can be as screwed up as the next man.'

Wriggling, Sorrel relaxed onto his sleek, hot body, shivering as the powerful and resilient length hardened beneath her. Her breath came fast through her lips, but although loving was wonderful, this quiet conversation was vital.

'Stop that,' he said, eyes possessive and hungry. 'I need to tell you this.'

She gave him a teasing, tender smile. 'All right. I think we'd got to the stage where you were going to explain why you behaved like a case history from a handbook for tyrants and despots that last summer at Parenga. Before you kissed me, that is.'

'Because even if I hadn't had a hang-up as big as Mt Cook I couldn't have asked a kid of eighteen to marry me, or even wait for me. Apart from the fact that you deserved a life of your own, all I had to offer was a run-down station that was going to take years of hard work to get back into any sort of shape. So I had to keep my distance.'

'Why did you kiss me?'

He gave her a grim smile. 'Because I couldn't help myself. You smiled up at me, and I gave up.'

'So you found a way to warn me off,' she said sadly, wishing she'd known all this then. It would have saved her so much heartache.

'Mari was a godsend; she gave me an excuse to pull back, to regroup, to convince myself that I was fine, it was only a temporary madness, one I'd soon get over.'

'I thought that too,' she said soberly. 'In fact, I was certain of it. Yet I kept you like a talisman at the back of my mind; I measured other men by you, and they all failed the test.'

'Idiots, both of us,' he said sombrely, turning his face into the warm curve of her throat. 'If I hadn't been so sure that loving you would make me humiliatingly dependent, we might have been able to work something out.'

'I was too young.'

'I know. And I was too angry with my father, too disgusted by Cherie to make any sort of commitment.' He kissed the beating hollow at the base of her throat, smiling at her response. Easing her sideways, he ran his hand across the slight curves of her breasts, cupping one to tease the nipple with his thumb.

Sorrel's pulse-rate soared. More than anything she wanted to forget everything in the honeyed fire of oblivion, but this was too important to rush through. She contented herself with nipping the rounded swell of a shoulder muscle, then sucked delicately on the smooth, hot skin.

His voice turned rough. 'I dreamed about you during those years. That final ad campaign haunted me—I wondered if you and the model were lovers, and I hated feeling vulnerable.'

'Luke—'

He interrupted with abrupt aloofness. 'No, let me get this out. I'm not going to ask about your lovers; it's none of my business.'

'And I have no intention of asking you how many lovers you've had,' she told him with a steely note in her voice.

'Probably fewer than you think.'

She looked him straight in the eyes. 'Likewise!'

His smile was twisted. 'By the time you came back I'd finished with Mari and accepted that I was going to have to deal with the way you affected me. I was in a filthy temper before you got here, but the reality of you, and the feel of you in my arms that first night at Parenga, sent me straight to hell. When Mari rang to ask if I was still taking her to that bloody premiere I ran like a coward; she sounded sensible and normal and I was torn by desires and needs I'd renounced years ago.'

He slid his fingers into her hair, letting it ripple through them in a fiery flood of red-brown silk. 'And it got worse. I started to wake every morning feeling that the only thing that validated each day was your presence. I was getting closer and closer to the abject adoration I despised in my father.'

Sorrel rested her cheek on his shoulder. 'But you don't feel like that now?' She held her breath.

He shook his head. 'It simply doesn't matter any more,' he said with calm conviction. 'I need you as much as I need to breathe. As for distrusting you—the first thing you did was risk your life for a cat. That was when I realised I was in real danger, so I tried to re-inforce all my defences by taking another leaf out of that handbook for tyrants and despots.' He gave an un-amused laugh. 'For all the good it did me!'

'It doesn't matter,' she murmured. 'It's the past, and the past is over; we own the future now.'

His fingers tightened in her hair; very gently he turned her head and tilted her face so that he could see it. 'When do you want to get married?' he asked casually, but his gaze was keen and intent.

'Are you sure?' she asked, searching his eyes.

'Absolutely.' He stretched like a great cat, tawny skin rippling, then kissed her. 'And the sooner the better,' he said against her lips in a voice velvet with pleasure.

'Can you still get married in three days here?'

He laughed. 'Yes, but you know, I think I'd like to marry you with all the pomp and ceremony I can manage. How about in a month's time?'

EPILOGUE

THEY were married in the garden at Parenga, beneath the magnolia. The bride wore ivory silk satin in a slender classical style with a small train, the South Sea pearls Luke had given her the night before, and the lace veil her mother had worn at her own wedding.

Her matron of honour was her best friend, Emma Talbot, whose amber dress hid the slight evidence of her second pregnancy. Kane, her tall, harsh-featured husband, gave the bride away.

Sorrel's goddaughter Cressy made a delicious little flower girl; once her father surrendered the bride to Luke, she curled up in his lap and watched the rest of the service with wide, dark eyes.

The guests were mainly local, although a couple of slender, gorgeous creatures with exotic accents had winged in from overseas to cut a swathe through the male guests. One incredibly handsome man was recognised as the model who'd starred with the bride in her final campaign; there was flutter of regret amongst the women when they realised his partner was another equally handsome male.

Sorrel's radiant face brought lumps to many throats, as did Luke's tenderness. The reception, a very cheerful affair, was held at Waimanu, and as they left for their honeymoon they were showered with rose petals.

They spent the first night at Luke's beach house on an offshore island. As they walked along the deserted beach, with the sunset filling the sky with a glory of gold and rose and orange, Sorrel said drily, 'I hope seeing Jason and Raoul together convinced you not to worry about those perfume ads. They're a very committed couple.'

'Nice guys,' he said, adding with an amused smile, 'I'm sure they suspected you were marrying some bone-headed hick, if their relief when they saw Waimanu was anything to go by. Last night they gave me a gentle grilling about my financial and emotional status—a follow-up to the one Kane put me through.'

He waited for her delighted gurgle of laughter, and when it was over finished smoothly, 'I think I managed to convince them all that I could keep you in silk and good food, and that I was reasonably good husband material.'

'The best,' she said immediately, smiling up at him.

Luke stopped and pulled her into his arms. 'I love you,' he said fiercely into her hair. 'But you know that now, don't you?'

She kissed his throat. 'I have a pretty good idea,' she murmured, heart swelling with joy.

He lifted her hand and gently bit the mound of Venus under her thumb. As little rills of pleasure ran through her, he said, 'I will always love you, and I know you're nothing like either my mother or Cherie—I don't know how I managed to persuade myself you might be.'

His mother had attended the wedding with her husband. A thin, brittle socialite, she'd watched her son with something like despairing hunger. Sorrel felt sorry for her, and intended to keep in touch.

But now was not the time to make plans. 'Nobody likes to feel they're a slave to their emotions.'

Luke tilted her face up and said quietly, 'Control's

always been important for me. Then you came along, and it shattered into a million pieces.'

He looked at her with naked longing, the strong framework of his face prominent beneath taut tanned skin. 'I didn't want to be like my father, caught in a relationship where I was the importunate one, the one who needed. But I didn't realise what I was asking from you—when you said you wouldn't accept an unequal relationship I realised that I was like Cherie, demanding all and giving nothing.'

'You are not like Cherie,' Sorrel said fiercely, trying to shake him and unable to move him at all. 'It's not like that for us—we're equals in everything.' She summoned a smile. 'Except in physical strength.'

'I love you, and you love me,' he said intensely. 'That's all that matters.'

He kissed her forehead, the tips of her eyebrows and the lobes of her ears; secure at last, she relaxed into him.

'I wonder how Cynthia knew,' Sorrel murmured, pushing aside his collar to punctuate the sentence with a little nip between each word.

When their engagement had been announced, the trustees for Parenga had sent her papers for dissolving the trust, with a letter from Cynthia. In her message Cynthia had said that she'd insisted on the six months' residency because she was sure that Sorrel and Luke were made for each other.

'She was a wise old bird,' Luke said, his voice thickening as her eager mouth moved slowly across his chest. 'What will you do with Parenga?'

She lifted her head to say, 'I think it would be a wonderful place for people to stay when they've been ill—families with sick children, perhaps.'

'My darling, kind-hearted Sorrel,' he said, his voice deep and tender. 'We'll work it out together later. At the moment I want you so much…'

'And I want you,' she said in a smoky, sensuous voice. 'Let's go up to the house.'

Together at last, safe in their love, they walked through the glory of the sunset into their future.

Modern Romance™
...seduction and
passion guaranteed

Tender Romance™
...love affairs that
last a lifetime

Sensual Romance™
...sassy, sexy and
seductive

Blaze Romance™
...the temperature's
rising

Medical Romance™
...medical drama on
the pulse

Historical Romance™
...rich, vivid and
passionate

27 new titles every month.

*With all kinds of Romance for
every kind of mood...*

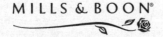

MILLS & BOON®

MB2

MILLS & BOON®

Modern Romance™

A PASSIONATE MARRIAGE by Michelle Reid

Hot-Blooded Husbands... Greek tycoon Leandros
Petronades married Isobel on the crest of a wild affair.
But within a year the marriage crashed and burned.
Three years on, Leandros comes face to face with
Isobel again and finds their all-consuming mutual
attraction is as strong as ever...

THE MARRIAGE TRUCE by Sara Craven

The bridesmaid's in love – with the best man!
Jenna is happy to be her cousin's bridesmaid, but she
wishes someone had warned her that the best man is
dynamic Ross Grantham – the man she once exchanged
marriage vows with in the very same church!

KEEPING LUKE'S SECRET by Carole Mortimer

Carole Mortimer's 115th book! When Leonie
meets the enigmatic Luke Richmond he takes an instant
dislike to her, and repeatedly asks her to leave. But he's
hiding something and Leonie's not going anywhere until
she finds out more...

THE PARISIAN PLAYBOY by Helen Brooks

**Getting down to business in the boardroom –
and the bedroom!** When Jacques Querruel decided
he wanted shy Holly Stanton as his personal secretary,
Holly fully intended not to be swept off her feet. But
being whisked away to Jacques's Paris penthouse,
working long hours by his side, she was bombarded
with temptation!

On sale 7th February 2003

*Available at most branches of WH Smith,
Tesco, Martins, Borders, Eason, Sainsbury's
and all good paperback bookshops.*

1202/01a

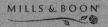

Modern Romance™

ON THE TYCOON'S TERMS *by Sandra Field*

Mistress – on his terms Luke McRae was a magnet for women, but no one had managed to break the control he had over his heart – until he met beautiful and vulnerable Katrin Sigurdson. Sharing a bed with Katrin was one thing. But allowing her into his life was quite another...

CONSTANTINOU'S MISTRESS *by Cathy Williams*

Sleeping with her Greek tycoon boss! After things got steamy with Lucy Reid and her gorgeous Greek boss Nick Constantinou they'd both vowed to go on as if nothing had happened. But now that Nick had discovered the passion that lay beneath Lucy's prim exterior, he could think of nothing else!

HIS CONVENIENT PROPOSAL *by Lindsay Armstrong*

Emotional rescue. The sexual tension between Ellie and gorgeous doctor Brett Spencer is overwhelming, but she is dismayed when he proposes a marriage of convenience. How can she marry a man she is sure will never love her while she is so desperately in love with him?

THE HEIRESS TAKES A HUSBAND *by Cara Colter*

She has one year to find a husband! Brittany Patterson has just inherited her own business. So what if she has to marry to keep it? She is determined to have it all – starting with the irresistible lawyer she's set her eyes on!

On sale 7th February 2003

Available at most branches of WH Smith, Tesco, Martins, Borders, Eason, Sainsbury's and all good paperback bookshops.

1202/01b

MILLS & BOON

Helen Brooks

Lynne Graham

Kim Lawrence

BUSINESS *Affairs*

Three brand-new stories about falling for the boss

Available from 17th January 2003

*Available at most branches of WH Smith,
Tesco, Martins, Borders, Eason, Sainsbury's
and all good paperback bookshops.*

0203/24/MB62

MILLS & BOON®

Modern Romance™

...seduction and passion guaranteed

We're on the lookout for HOT new authors...

Think you have what it takes to write a novel?

Then this is your chance!

Can you create:

A proud, passionate and hot-blooded hero that no woman could resist? He has everything – except a woman to share it with...

A sexy and successful contemporary heroine, who can take on the ultimate man on her own terms?

Could you transport readers into a sophisticated international world of tantalizing romantic excitement where seduction and passion are guaranteed?

If so, we want to hear from you!

Visit www.millsandboon.co.uk for editorial guidelines.

Submit the first three chapters and synopsis to:
Harlequin Mills & Boon Editorial Department,
Eton House, 18-24 Paradise Road,
Richmond, Surrey, TW9 1SR,
United Kingdom.

0103/WRITERS/MOD

LR7022   GL832

2 FREE

books and a surprise gift!

We would like to take this opportunity to thank you for reading this Mills & Boon® book by offering you the chance to take TWO more specially selected titles from the Modern Romance™ series absolutely FREE! We're also making this offer to introduce you to the benefits of the Reader Service™—

- ★ FREE home delivery
- ★ FREE gifts and competitions
- ★ FREE monthly Newsletter
- ★ Exclusive Reader Service discount
- ★ Books available before they're in the shops

Accepting these FREE books and gift places you under no obligation to buy, you may cancel at any time, even after receiving your free shipment. Simply complete your details below and return the entire page to the address below. *You don't even need a stamp!*

YES! Please send me 2 free Modern Romance books and a surprise gift. I understand that unless you hear from me, I will receive 4 superb new titles every month for just £2.55 each, postage and packing free. I am under no obligation to purchase any books and may cancel my subscription at any time. The free books and gift will be mine to keep in any case.

P3ZEA

Ms/Mrs/Miss/Mr ....Initials...............................
BLOCK CAPITALS PLEASE

Surname ....

Address ....

....

....Postcode...............................

Send this whole page to:
UK: FREEPOST CN81, Croydon, CR9 3WZ
EIRE: PO Box 4546, Kilcock, County Kildare (stamp required)

Offer valid in UK and Eire only and not available to current Reader Service subscribers to this series. We reserve the right to refuse an application and applicants must be aged 18 years or over. Only one application per household. Terms and prices subject to change without notice. Offer expires 30th April 2003. As a result of this application, you may receive offers from Harlequin Mills & Boon and other carefully selected companies. If you would prefer not to share in this opportunity please write to The Data Manager at the address above.

Mills & Boon® is a registered trademark owned by Harlequin Mills & Boon Limited. Modern Romance™ is being used as a trademark.